SPECIAL MESSAGE TO READERS

THE ULVERSCROFT FOUNDATION
(registered UK charity number 264873)
was established in 1972 to provide funds for
research, diagnosis and treatment of eye diseases.
Examples of major projects funded by
the Ulverscroft Foundation are:-

- The Children's Eye Unit at Moorfields Eye Hospital, London
- The Ulverscroft Children's Eye Unit at Great Ormond Street Hospital for Sick Children
- Funding research into eye diseases and treatment at the Department of Ophthalmology, University of Leicester
- The Ulverscroft Vision Research Group, Institute of Child Health
- Twin operating theatres at the Western Ophthalmic Hospital, London
- The Chair of Ophthalmology at the Royal Australian College of Ophthalmologists

You can help further the work of the Foundation
by making a donation or leaving a legacy.
Every contribution is gratefully received. If you
would like to help support the Foundation or
require further information, please contact:

THE ULVERSCROFT FOUNDATION
The Green, Bradgate Road, Anstey
Leicester LE7 7FU, England
Tel: (0116) 236 4325

website: www.foundation.ulverscroft.com

CLIFF HOUSE

When Cliff House, which Jazz loved to visit as a child, is left to her by her Aunt Emily, she decides to move in rather than sell. It isn't long, however, before she's wondering if that decision was the right one, as mysterious and disturbing events lead her to question her very sanity. Or is it all just the cruel trickery of wealthy property developer Zak Rivers? And how can she stop herself from falling in love with the very last man she can ever trust?

SUSAN UDY

CLIFF HOUSE

Complete and Unabridged

LINFORD
Leicester

First published in Great Britain in 2013

First Linford Edition
published 2014

A catalogue record for this book is available
from the British Library.

ISBN 978–1–4448–2120–8

Published by
F. A. Thorpe (Publishing)
Anstey, Leicestershire

Set by Words & Graphics Ltd.
Anstey, Leicestershire
Printed and bound in Great Britain by
T. J. International Ltd., Padstow, Cornwall

This book is printed on acid-free paper

1

There it was again, the sound of footsteps.

Jazz Wheatley lifted her gaze from the page of the book she'd been reading to stare up at the ceiling of the sitting room. This was the third evening in a row that she'd heard it — at exactly the same time. It was as if someone was walking across the floor of the guest room immediately above her.

Initially, she'd told herself that it was simply the noises that an old house made, but now she questioned that theory. She'd swear they were footsteps, moving regularly and steadily across the floor — totally unlike the random creaking that ancient floorboards made.

She put her book down and stood up, tilting her head, intently listening for any further sounds. There couldn't be someone up there. It was impossible, she was alone here. And, in any case, how would anyone have got into the house? As soon as it had grown dark, she'd locked all the doors and closed any windows that had still been open, paying special attention to the small pantry window that refused to shut completely, no matter what she did — although that was too small for anyone, other than a small child, to get through. And she'd have heard the sound of someone breaking in.

Barely breathing, she waited for the next footfall: it didn't come. Exactly as had happened before, it had all stopped as suddenly as it had started.

Quickly, and before her courage could desert her, she swept from the room and up the stairs, stopping halfway up to listen once more. Nothing; the house was completely silent. More confident now that she wouldn't be confronting an intruder once she reached the landing, she carried on and headed for the bedroom from where she believed the sounds had been coming. She flung open the door. The room was empty — just as it had been when she'd checked both times before. She moved further into the bedroom — it was the largest of the three guest rooms — and stood gazing around. Nothing was out of place; the room was exactly as it should be. She even went so far as to open the wardrobe door this time and look inside. Of course, it too was empty. What had she expected — to find someone crouching inside?

She gave a snort of derision at her foolishness and returned to the sitting room where she instantly switched on the radio. Music poured out, one of Beethoven's piano sonatas, she thought. She turned the volume up before sitting down again; there — that would drown out any further inexplicable noises.

For heaven's sake, she mutely chastised herself, did she never learn? She'd always been the same, letting her imagination run riot. As a child, it had been the bane of her and her family's life. She'd lie in bed at night, the sheet dragged up over her nose, eyes wide with fear as she stared over it. A shadow in the corner of her bedroom turned into a monster, a sweater draped over a chair was transformed into a person sitting there — watching her, waiting till she was asleep to pounce, a dropped sock curled into the shape of a snake on the floor. As a consequence, her screams regularly woke the entire household.

However, she was no longer a child, so she'd simply have to get used to the unfamiliar creaks and groans of the old house. Either that or do as her sister was urging and move back to her modern flat in Worcestershire. She knew of at least two other people who'd welcome that decision.

And with that, her thoughts reverted to the phone call that had informed her of her Aunt Emily's death, the subsequent funeral, and then the meeting with the elderly solicitor who'd handled her aunt's affairs.

The initial call had come completely out of the blue. A woman, who had announced herself as a close friend of Emily's, had tearfully informed her of her aunt's death.

Jazz had been so shocked that she hadn't been able to speak at first. Then, she'd managed to stammer, 'B-but I didn't know she'd even been ill? Wh-why didn't she call me?'

'She hadn't been ill, that's the tragedy of it. She had a sudden, massive heart attack.'

'No! Oh God — ' Grief had literally swamped Jazz.

'You'll attend the funeral?'

'Of course I will.'

Jazz had replaced the phone, her hand shaking so badly she missed the base altogether to start with. How could this have happened? How could she have let it happen? She'd always thought she'd have time to put things right between them all. Now . . . now, it was too late. With a hand that still shook, she dialled her parents' phone number in Spain where they had lived for the last couple of years, but there was no response. She tried her sister's number next. Felicity, the eldest by two years and who from the age of six had refused to answer to any other name but Flick, had sounded as shocked as Jazz, but their parents, despite several phone calls over the next few days, had remained unreachable. Why didn't they get a computer, she fumed, so they could keep in touch by email — or, at the very least, an answering machine?

For Serena and Brad, Jazz's parents, had decamped to Spain once Brad had decided to retire, Serena deciding that the climate would suit her better than the fickle English weather.

However, this failure to contact them meant that Jazz and Flick were forced to make the journey south to attend Emily's funeral, and then to subsequently see the solicitor who'd handled the dead woman's affairs, all without the comforting presence of their parents.

Thus it was that Jazz found herself staring at the elderly man sitting on the opposite side of the desk to her, too shocked to properly assimilate what the solicitor had just told them. Flick, equally as stunned, gasped at her side, 'What?' Whatever they'd expected to hear today, it hadn't been this.

'As well as the bequest to you, Mrs Matthews,' he glanced at Flick, 'a very substantial twenty thousand pounds — as I've just said the rest of the estate, in its entirety, goes to you, Ms Wheatley.'

'Wait,' Flick cried then, 'don't I get a share in the house?'

The solicitor smiled fleetingly at her. 'I'm afraid not.' He swept his gaze back to Jazz. 'As well as Cliff House and her business, your aunt has left you a considerable amount of money, both in her account and in the form of shares in various companies. You will be a relatively wealthy young woman. You will certainly inherit enough to maintain the house, should you so desire, for many years to come. However, there have been two offers to buy the property.' He glanced at a separate sheet of paper on his desk. 'They are from Zak Rivers of Rivers Corporation and Blake Carlisle of South Western Enterprises. Both have offered considerable sums — ' He passed a piece of paper to Jazz. She looked at it and her eyes widened. The house couldn't possibly be worth that much. So why were they offering such a lot? Rivers Corporation was offering just under a million pounds, the other, South Western Enterprises, three quarters of a million. 'You will see I have also written down their respective phone numbers so that you, yourself, can contact them if you wish. They will each be in touch with you, I'm sure.'

Jazz folded the piece of paper and slipped it into her handbag, disregarding her sister's demanding glare. Now wasn't the time to discuss this, or — as was much more likely, knowing her sister as she did — argue about it. That would have to come later. She wasn't prepared to embark upon any sort of discussion in the presence of the solicitor. In any case, shock had rendered her momentarily incapable of thought, let alone speech.

Somehow, she ignored the waves of resentment and fury that were now emanating from her sister towards her and managed a calm goodbye to the solicitor. Such heated emotion was understandable, she supposed. In the event of any bequest, Flick, who was also Emily's niece, would have expected to inherit equally with Jazz. Apart from their mother, Emily's sister, Jazz and Flick were their aunt's sole family. What neither of them had expected was that Jazz would be the main beneficiary.

'I want to go and see the house first. It's been many years since I last visited — ' somewhere in the region of sixteen years, actually. She'd been seven, nearly eight, that last time. Not surprisingly, her recollections of the house were hazy. What she did recall — with startling clarity — was her aunt.

Her smile, the way her eyes lit up with love, the way she'd swing Jazz up into her arms — Jazz's eyes stung with tears, as the memories, the images, all came flooding back. Flick had steadfastly refused to accompany her on any of her visits, so Jazz had had her aunt all to herself. It had resulted in an extremely close and loving relationship. It had also inspired a fervent desire to, one day, go and live at Cliff House. Her aunt had always promised that she would — 'one day, darling; one day.' And now, astonishingly, she'd kept that promise. The only thing was — Jazz had wanted to live there with her aunt, not alone in the wake of Emily's death. And she certainly hadn't expected to be left practically everything.

'Well, of course,' the solicitor murmured, 'it's your house — '

Yes, that's right — it was, Jazz mused. What would she do with a house miles away from Worcestershire where she lived and worked? It would have been different if her aunt had still been alive.

Jazz regarded the solicitor anxiously then. 'So — my mother, Serena, isn't mentioned in the will?'

'I'm afraid not, just you and your sister.'

Why Jazz should be surprised by that she didn't know. Serena and Emily had quarrelled years ago. It was the reason that Jazz had stopped visiting her aunt. She frowned. To this day, she had no idea what had caused the row, but it had been serious enough to prevent any further contact between the two sisters, and, as a result, between Jazz and Emily, too. Mind you, Jazz hadn't accepted the cessation of her visits without a great deal of protest — even at the age of seven. But Serena had been adamant. 'I don't want to hear that woman's name mentioned ever again in this house.'

Jazz had, however, unbeknownst to either of her parents, used some of her pocket money and managed to send regular postcards, birthday and Christmas cards, so that her aunt always knew her whereabouts. She'd felt bad about not seeing her, especially as she'd grown older and could have travelled alone. But that would have felt like a betrayal of her mother, so, instead, she'd contented herself with postal contact and the occasional phone call, always hoping that someday, in the not too distant future, the rift could be mended. Now, it never would be.

Jazz felt an overwhelming guilt. Emily had never once complained, not in all the years that had gone by. But whatever had happened between the two sisters, Emily had remembered her promise to a little girl and left Jazz her house, a pretty substantial house, a million pounds worth of house if the offer from Zak Rivers was anything to go by.

She dimly remembered it as being a double fronted, grey walled building, with plenty of space for a small girl with an over-active imagination to hide in, to play games in, and to search for hidden treasure in. Or was that simply a child's memory playing tricks? It might not seem so large now that she was an adult.

She and Flick had booked themselves into a small hotel right in the centre of St. Kernan that overlooked an estuary that in the summer months would be packed with yachts and boats. Now, at the end of October, it was virtually empty. They returned there after seeing the solicitor, with Jazz trying very hard not to listen to the ranting of her sister.

'I can't believe what's happened,' Flick cried. 'That you've had everything — I was relying on that money, I knew there must be quite a lot. And with her and Mum not speaking, who else would she leave it to but you and me?'

'Well, I suppose that's what she's done,' Jazz replied absently.

'Huh! Really — so who's got the lion's share then? Not me, that's for sure. It's just not fair — ' she wailed.

'Well, maybe if you'd visited her like I did, you'd have built the same sort of relationship, but you always refused — '

13

Jazz suddenly stared at her sister. 'What do you mean? You were relying on that money? You couldn't have been expecting her to die this young — She was only fifty one.'

Flick looked uncomfortable. 'I mean — since we heard.' Her face had reddened.

'What have you done, Flick?' Jazz eyed her sister.

'We-ell,' Flick's colour deepened, 'there were things Gary and I needed — '

'What things?'

'New clothes, bills to pay — items for the house, you know. We haven't been able to afford much since we got married — it's been difficult. Gary had to take a wage cut — what with the recession and everything. We haven't even had a holiday.'

Jazz's gaze remained steady; steely, even.

'I — um, I put some of it onto my credit cards, and . . . and borrowed the rest — ' Flick looked down at the ground.

'How much have you borrowed — altogether?'

'Forty grand's worth — give or take,' Flick mumbled.

'Forty — ' Jazz gasped, completely lost for words. She knew her sister could be impulsive, but this was mind bogglingly impulsive. 'So — how much, give or take, are you talking about exactly?' Her voice had hardened, until it was as steely as her eyes had been.

'Forty four — '

'How could you have been so stupid? You had no idea how much Emily was worth, what she had to leave. Or who she would leave it to, come to that. And there might not have been any money at all. Had you considered that?'

'Of course I knew there'd be money. Just take her business; it must have made a fortune. You were always seeing her advertisements in the glossy magazines, and they don't come cheap. And then, there was the house. Who else would she leave it all to, the cat's home? I hardly think so.' She eyed her sister, her expression one of calculation and greed. 'How much have you been offered for Cliff House?'

'A million — ' Jazz gnawed at her bottom lip. Damn! She'd intended to be a little more circumspect about sharing that information with Flick — just until she'd worked out what she wanted to do with regards to the house.

Her sister, just as she'd anticipated, reacted immediately. 'What — a million? Wow! I didn't expect that — ' her expression instantly darkened. 'Does that seem fair to you? That you stand to have all that, plus whatever you sell the business for? And then there's shares — You should give me half of everything.'

But Jazz wasn't about to be bullied into anything. She'd had enough of that in their younger years. If Flick hadn't been able to get what she wanted — instantly, she'd scream and shout hysterically at her smaller sister, at times even resorting to pinching and slapping. With that in mind — not that she really thought that Flick would hit her — Jazz spoke this time with considerably more caution. 'I don't know what I want to do yet — whether I'll sell or live here.'

'You can't live here — on your own. You have to sell it; you just have to.' Her voice rose. 'How am I going to pay off the debts if you don't give me the money? I told Gary there'd be no problem — you have to help me; you have to. You don't need all that money — you're so selfish — '

Flick was so like their mother, Serena, Jazz reflected. They both thought the world revolved around them. They even looked alike: full breasted and curvaceous; both blonde, with delicate china-doll features and melting blue eyes that very effectively disguised a tenacious determination to have their own way in all things, and that usually ensured they got it. It was all so completely different to Jazz's gentle nature, her hazel eyes and freckled nose, her shoulder length, caramel-coloured hair and slender, modestly breasted figure.

Flick had married Gary six months ago and Jazz wasn't sure if he was much more level headed. He couldn't be, if he let Flick blow forty four grand on the dubious prospect of a large inheritance.

'Well, whatever I decide to do, you'll have the twenty grand — ' she quietly pointed out.

'But it'll still leave twenty four thousand owing and — anyway,' Flick's glance sharpened, 'how long will the money take to come through? I need some — right now.'

Jazz shrugged. 'I've no idea. However much you inherited, you'd probably still have to wait for it. These things take time — Maybe dad could help you out with a loan till things are sorted?'

Flick looked slightly mollified at that idea. 'Yeah, I'll ask him — but you'll help me out as well, won't you — if you sell the house?'

Jazz didn't say anything. She wasn't about to make any promises until she saw for herself — never mind what the solicitor had said — the exact state of Emily's finances and had worked out how much she'd need for the future upkeep of Cliff House. She stopped right there — when had she made that decision — to keep the house? She didn't know; she hadn't consciously done so, but what she did know was that she wasn't going to rush into anything. She needed time to think everything through, assess the condition of the house, and whether she could, in reality, live there alone. Until then everything was on hold — no matter what Flick argued.

'You will, won't you, Jazz?' Flick urged her.

'I don't know, Flick; I simply don't know — '

* * *

They had lunch in the hotel and afterwards made their way to Cliff House. Jazz had forgotten how far from

St. Kernan it was, and how steeply the road rose out of the town. It narrowed sharply as it left the last of the houses behind and Cliff House stood another mile or so on, right on the cliff top — as the name indicated — at the start of a small promontory that partially sheltered the harbour of St. Kernan from the power of the sea and the fearsome winds that could at times arise out of nowhere. Of course, it meant that the house suffered the occasional battering as the gales blew in — well, more than occasionally if she remembered it rightly, even in summer — but its walls were solidly built and parts of it had stood now for three hundred years, so Jazz wasn't particularly concerned.

On the other side of this promontory lay a large bay and another town, Porth Brennan. This was more of a resort than St. Kernan and contained several hotels as well as a couple of substantial holiday parks on its edge. According to the solicitor, these were owned by South Western Enterprises.

The house, when they reached it, looked just as Jazz remembered it; a little smaller, perhaps, but still a reasonably sized house. The garden in front was tidier than she recalled. It split in two, continuing along both sides of the building to merge again and form a huge rear garden. This stretched as far as the cliff edge, along which ran an unobtrusive wire and wooden post fence. There was nothing to block the marvellous views. In all, there was a good two to three acres of land, she estimated, most of it running along the cliff top. It was mostly lawn, so the maintenance of it shouldn't be too onerous. There she went again. Thinking — planning — as if she were going to live here, when really she hadn't definitely decided. Or had she?

She opened the front door with the key that the solicitor had given her; and she and Flick stepped into a hallway that looked very different to when she'd last been here. Natural stone now covered what had once been a rather worn parquet floor and antique furniture had replaced the pine cupboards and shelves that had lined the walls years ago. Although one tall cupboard remained — to hang coats in. A burred walnut table sat plump in the centre, and a gently curving staircase led up to the four bedrooms. Three doors opened off the hallway, into a kitchen, a dining room and a spacious sitting room. The ceiling of the hall was heavily beamed; the wood was stained a more natural-looking light oak now, rather than the slightly oppressive black that Jazz remembered. Flick was correct, Emily's interior design business had clearly been extremely profitable, and from all the evidence before them, she had lavished a generous portion of those profits upon her home.

Eagerly now, Jazz threw open the door that lay straight ahead and which she remembered led into the kitchen. This also had been transformed with marble worktops and very expensive-looking, limed oak cupboards on three of the walls, although the small walk-in pantry had survived the renovation. The fourth wall consisted of a window that overlooked the sea and an alcove containing a massive Aga. Copper jelly moulds and strings of onions and garlic flanked this. There was also a built-in electric oven and a central island containing a hob and a sink. Stools lined the one side of this to form a breakfast bar. The floor was covered in terracotta tiles.

'Wow!' Flick gasped, her anger with her sister forgotten for the moment, or if not forgotten, at least put to one side. 'This is my dream kitchen. No wonder you've been offered a million — '

Jazz didn't reveal by as much as a glimmer that the more she saw of the house, the more she wanted to live in it.

'Come on,' Flick cried, 'let's have a look at the rest.'

The next room they went into was the dining room. This, in contrast to the kitchen, had changed very little over the years. The walls were still oak panelled, and the burgundy red carpet looked the same, giving it a cosy, familiar feel. Jazz had had a habit of running her fingers all over the wood as a little girl — well, as far as she could reach — excitedly looking for a secret passage. Of course, she'd never found one. A long table sat centrally, with eight high-backed chairs around it. A bulky sideboard lay against one wall, over which hung a large oil painting. Crammed into a corner was an upright piano. Jazz smiled to herself. She'd spent many a happy hour trying to emulate her aunt on it. Emily had been an accomplished pianist, certainly proficient enough to have performed in public had she so wished.

The sitting room, again totally transformed from the way Jazz remembered it, was a delight, with a light oak floor, scattered rugs, and sumptuous, cream upholstered furniture. This was heaped with brightly coloured cushions. An inglenook fireplace practically filled one side of the room, containing a large log burner, and a pile of cut logs, ready for burning, to one side of it. Watercolour paintings decorated the honey coloured walls, and full length, apricot and cream silk curtains flanked the windows, generously bunching on the floor, bestowing the impression of luxury and wealth. Emily had made full use of her undoubted talent and created a home that was stylishly comfortable.

'Well,' Flick commented, 'from the look of all of this, there wasn't any shortage of money.'

Jazz ignored the insensitivity of that remark, although she couldn't help the tears that sprang into her eyes. She'd give everything she was about to possess to have her aunt walk into the room right now and give her a hug.

They climbed the stairs to discover that the bedrooms were all equally as comfortable. En-suite shower rooms had been added to the two largest ones, supplementing the main bathroom. As Flick had said, Emily had clearly done very well in her business. The remainder of the estate would surely more than provide for Jazz to remain here — especially if she sold Emily's business and some of the shares that she had accumulated. Flick was right. The business would fetch a considerable sum.

Flick and Jazz returned to the hotel, both wrapped up in their respective thoughts. Not unexpectedly, dinner that evening was a relatively subdued affair. Flick did eventually ask, 'You are going to sell the house, aren't you?'

Jazz didn't answer.

That night, she dreamed. She was a child again, staying at Cliff House with her aunt. They were playing in the garden.

'Come on,' her aunt said. 'Daddy will be here soon. We need to get you packed — '

'I don't want to go home. I want to stay here with you.'

'Jazz, darling, I would love you to but what would Mummy and Daddy do without you?'

Suddenly, in the way of dreams, her

father was there. He disappeared into the house with Emily. Jazz continued to play quite happily in the garden. When her aunt and father returned to her, they looked strange. Her aunt's eyes were bright, and shiny, her cheeks flushed. Her father had looked serious — It had been the last time she'd visited.

She awoke with a start. Something had happened between them that day — something that had altered — no — spoilt everything.

2

But come the next morning, Jazz's thoughts were a seething mix of uncertainty and deep sadness. If being able to live in Cliff House meant losing her aunt, then she'd relinquish the opportunity in a second. For her dream had unearthed long forgotten memories of Emily and her holidays at Cliff House. In fact, everything had been so graphically clear that it effectively did away with any hope of sleep for the rest of the night, which meant she was heartily relieved when daylight broke, and she could get up, dress herself, and go outside to her car. Half an hour later she was at Cliff House, standing, staring at the exterior of the building that now belonged to her. Flick wouldn't wake for another hour or so and begin to wonder where she was, which meant she had time to look round the house on her own — something she'd longed to do the day before.

Despite the early morning cloud and a distinctly chill breeze, the air held the promise of a bright day. She decided to have a walk round the garden before going inside. She felt a sudden need to see the sea and listen to the waves smashing themselves against the rocks far below; she also needed the time to just stand and remember her aunt and the happy times they'd spent together here.

She pulled a fleece jacket from the back seat of the car and was slipping her arms into it when she heard something, someone clearing their throat, and it was coming from behind the house. Who could be here? It was only just after eight thirty, for heaven's sake. Way too early for any sort of social call.

She quickened her step and headed for the rear garden. To her annoyance, a man stood, exactly where she had intended standing, on the cliff edge, his back to her, as he gazed out to sea. He was dressed in jeans and a sweat shirt.

Who the hell was he? And what a cheek! Anyone would think he owned the place.

Belatedly apprehensive, Jazz stood absolutely still. Suppose he was up to no good? Suppose he knew the house was empty and was here, preparing to break in? But — would he hang around in the garden first, taking the risk of being discovered? Surely he'd just get on with it and make a quick getaway? She began to back away, intending to return to her car and call the police, but something must have alerted him to the fact that he was no longer alone, because he whirled to face her.

Her apprehension turned to alarm then. There was something very intimidating about him; menacing, even. Her fears seemed realised; he was up to no good. This impression was intensified when he stared at her from beneath a tangle of dark hair, his eyebrows lowered into a frown over a pair of inky eyes. The shape of his nose only added to his air of menace, it was crooked, as if it had been broken at some time, and his jaw was so sharply defined it could have sliced paper. Add to all of that, the fact that he was tall, six feet two or three, she'd guess, and powerfully built, and you had someone that she, for one, wouldn't want to tackle in any sort of confrontation.

Jazz took a deep breath and, hoping she sounded more confident than she felt, asked, 'Can I help you?'

He took a couple of long strides towards her, holding out his hand. 'You must be Ms Wheatley. I'm very sorry for your loss — And please accept my apologies for this intrusion. I didn't envisage anyone being here yet — '

'Well, I have to admit, it is bit of a surprise, finding I have a visitor this early. I . . . I didn't see a car.' She merely brushed his hand with the tips of her fingers. In fact, she'd been tempted to ignore it, but good manners triumphed.

'No, I don't have one with me. I have a run most mornings. I leave it parked in the town car park — I was passing Cliff House,' he did smile now, if you could call the slight quirk of his lips a smile. It didn't make him seem any less intimidating, 'and I was tempted into trespassing, I'm afraid. You must think me terribly impertinent.'

'I see, but who — ?'

'I apologise. I haven't introduced myself, have I? Zak Rivers.'

The man who'd made an offer to buy Cliff House; the same man who had many extremely profitable business interests and who lived on the other side of the town in an 18th century manor house, the only manor house in this area. A couple of discreet enquiries to the receptionist at the hotel had readily elicited this information. She'd then added, ' — 'e's a millionaire several times over — '

'I presume the solicitor told you of my offer to buy Cliff House in order to develop it.'

Jazz's head lifted. Develop it? This was the first she'd heard about that. 'Develop it — how, exactly?'

'Oh, didn't you know?'

'No, I didn't.' The solicitor hadn't mentioned it. Maybe he hadn't known either.

'That's why I've offered so much money for it. The house itself would be worth much less. I naturally assumed you'd realise that — '

His tone, as well as his single raised eyebrow, conveyed his contempt for her apparent stupidity.

'Uh, well — I did wonder — ' Jazz mumbled. Who the blazes did he think he was? Talking to her in such a manner? How would she have known how much the house was worth? She hadn't seen it in years.

'I'm planning to extend and adapt it to make it into a luxury, five star hotel. It would be the only one in this region, so I should recoup the high cost in a relatively short time. It's perfectly situated, the only house hereabouts that is — ' He waved a hand, indicating the grounds and the panoramic view of the sea. 'People will pay a premium for sea views, and I fully intend that every room and suite will have that benefit.'

Such was the absolute confidence of both his manner and expression that she suspected he was rarely refused anything. Well, that was about to change.

'Cliff House is not for sale,' she abruptly told him. And that was that, without as much as a second thought, her decision was made. This high and mighty individual was not going to have the opportunity to destroy the house that she loved. She would not sell, not for a million pounds, not for two million. Not for anything, in fact. He could build his hotel somewhere else.

He didn't at first respond, other than to stare at her, his eyebrows once more lowered over eyes that had lightened and turned steely. 'I've assumed you know how much I'm offering?'

'Yes, and I repeat — Cliff House is

not for sale, especially not to a developer.'

'So — what are you going to do with it then?'

'Do you know — I thought I might live in it.'

'I see.' He tilted his head to one side and continued to study her. He didn't seem to have registered her sarcasm, because his gaze was opaque and without expression of any sort. She had no idea what he was thinking, which was highly irritating. 'So-o, you're not going to sell to Carlisle then either? He's got even bigger plans for it. A luxury caravan park from what I've been hearing.'

'As I said, Cliff House is not for sale. Not now, not ever, not to anyone. Be they a private buyer or a developer.'

'How about if I up the offer, would that make it more acceptable?'

Thoroughly nettled now by the fact that not only did he deem her stupid, he also believed she was the type of person who could be bought for an extra few thousand pounds, she snapped, 'The price you're prepared to pay is irrelevant.'

'I see.' He continued to study her, looking in no way put out by her refusal to sell to him, which was slightly curious considering how keen he'd sounded to buy. 'Are you sure you know what you're letting yourself in for?'

'What do you mean?'

'Well, I heard that you're going to be living here alone.'

How the hell did he know that? She hadn't even told Flick yet what she'd decided. Or maybe he didn't know and was fishing for information? She suspected he was. Mind you, she mused, passing on gossip was the chief occupation in St. Kernan. Everyone knew everyone else's business. And what people didn't know, they made up — or so Emily had always maintained. It was beginning to look as if she'd been right.

'This is a very isolated house,' he

went on, 'I wondered if you were prepared for the loneliness? The winds? Even in the summer they can be pretty powerful.'

'Well, that worry hasn't stopped you planning a hotel in this very spot. Tell me — how do you think your guests will feel about a wind strong enough to blow them off their feet the moment they walk out of the door? Not quite what they'd be expecting in a — luxury hotel, I would imagine.'

He didn't respond to her jibe, other than for a tightening of his lips.

'My aunt had no problem with either the loneliness of her situation or the strength of the wind, and neither did I when I used to stay here as a child. So, what makes you think I will now? Be assured, I know exactly what I'll be taking on, Mr Rivers.'

'Oh, please, call me Zak.'

'Mr Rivers,' she made a point of emphasising the two words. If he believed that by inviting her to use his Christian name and so foster an illusion of friendship between them would make any difference to her decision then he could think again.

'Well,' he drawled, apparently undaunted by her refusal to do as he wanted, 'my guess would be that you're a city girl — '

'Then your guess would be wrong. I come from a town in Worcestershire.'

'Precisely — a town; a whole lot different to a place that's little bigger than a large village, in a house that's stuck out on its own, literally teetering on a cliff edge — '

'If you're trying to make me nervous, you won't succeed. As I've just told you, I was perfectly used to that. It didn't bother me as a child, and it certainly won't now. And Cliff House is not teetering on the cliff edge.'

'Maybe not, but with the coastal erosion that's promised along with climate change — ' he shrugged his shoulders, 'who's to say what the future holds? And just for your information, I'm not trying to make you nervous. I wouldn't be that irresponsible. I'm merely pointing out the drawbacks of living here — purely in your interests, of course.' He eyed her then for a moment or two. 'How old were you when you used to stay here?'

'From the age of four until I was seven — '

'Bit different to now then. You were a mere child and had company, that of an aunt who would have protected you.'

'Against what, Mr Rivers? I'm a grown woman, accustomed to looking after herself. So, I ask you again, protect me against what?'

Again, he shrugged. 'Oh, anything really: storms; intruders — '

'Intruders?' she exclaimed.

'Yes, there's always someone wanting what you've got — '

'Oh,' she cried, 'you mean someone like you, Mr Rivers?'

He gave a crack of laughter at that, not that there was much humour to be heard in it. 'I can see I've come up against a pretty formidable adversary.'

'If, by that, you mean that I won't be browbeaten or threatened into selling to you, then yes — '

His eyes narrowed at her. 'I have never browbeaten anyone in my life, and as for threatening a woman — '

He wasn't bothering to hide his annoyance with her, and perhaps she had been a little unfair. 'Well, I just want you to know that nothing you can say will persuade me to sell Cliff House.'

'Fine; it's your decision.' He paused. 'I presume I was right as you haven't contradicted me — you are going to be living alone?'

She curtly nodded and then promptly cursed her stupidity in letting him know that. She knew absolutely nothing about him, other than the fact that he was immensely rich. He could be some sort of criminal. The sort of wealth which he reputedly possessed was often accumulated from the proceeds of crime.

'And do you intend for things to stay that way?'

'Who knows?' Let him make what he wanted out of that. She wasn't about to give anything else away. She'd said quite enough already.

'Well, I will bid you farewell and continue with my run. I'm obviously not going to be able to persuade you to sell to me — not at the moment, at any rate.'

'Not at any other moment either, Mr Rivers,' she bit out.

He held up both of his hands, palms facing her, in a clear gesture of surrender. 'I get the message. However, in case you ever do decide — '

'Believe me, I won't.'

'If you ever do — ' he slid a hand into the pocket of his jeans, 'here's my card.'

Jazz had no option but to take it, as he was more or less thrusting it at her. He was persistent, she'd give him that.

'The offer will remain on the table for a while, and I will just say that anything Carlisle offers you, I'll better. I'd like you to remember that.'

Jazz didn't respond, other than to think — crikey! He was keen to get his hands on the house; too keen, maybe. Apprehension reared its head again, as she recalled how eager he'd been to find out whether she intended living here alone or not. And she'd told him she would be. How foolish, because she'd imagine he could be pretty ruthless when circumstances demanded. Even to the extent of maybe trying to frighten her into selling to him with that remark about intruders?

'Well, good to meet you, Ms Wheatley. I live on the other side of the town, in The Old Manor House.'

'Yes, I know.'

'Oh, you do, do you?' His expression told her that he'd guessed she'd been making enquiries about him. 'Well, in that case, if ever you're nearby, do call in. I'll crack open a bottle of wine.'

'Thanks, but I doubt I'll have the time — '

It wasn't until Jazz returned to Linford Green that she managed to contact her parents in Spain.

'Where have you been?' she demanded. 'I've been trying for days to talk to you. It's Emily — she's dead.' She bit her lip, annoyed at herself. There'd been no need to be so brutal. 'The funeral was on Tuesday.'

'Oh, my God!' Serena sounded unexpectedly shaken. Maybe she cared more about her sister than she'd ever admitted — despite their long estrangement. Her voice faded as she turned away from the mouthpiece. 'Emily's dead.'

Jazz's father broke in then. 'Emily's dead?'

'Yes,' Jazz's voice was beginning to wobble, 'a massive heart attack, a-and she left me Cliff House — everything, in fact, her business, her money — '

'We'll come straight back — '

'No, there's no need for that.'

'How's Flick taken it — the fact that you're sole inheritor?'

'Badly — she has been left some money.'

'Well, don't let her bully you into doing anything you don't want to.'

As she ended the phone call, Jazz found herself wondering if Flick's money troubles were really as bad as she had said. Her sister had been known to grossly exaggerate things in order to get her own way. However, if they were that bad, maybe Jazz should do as she wanted and, as soon as matters were finally settled with regards to the will, give her sister the money she needed to pay off her debts? She didn't want her own good fortune to cause a problem between them. One family split was one too many; two would be a tragedy.

All she had to do now was tell Flick that she had decided not to sell but to move to St. Kernan, and she wasn't looking forward to that, not one little bit.

And, sure enough, Flick reacted exactly as Jazz had expected. 'What about me,' she stormed, 'and my debts? Is it really fair that you get practically everything?'

Jazz patiently explained what she intended to do. It did appease her sister, somewhat. 'We-ell, okay, thanks. But what do you want to live down there for — in the back of beyond? You'll be miles away — '

'Flick, it's four — four and a half hours down the M5. It's hardly the other side of the world. Come and see me. Spend your holidays with me, you and Gary — I'll need some company now and again.'

Recollections of Zak Rivers' warnings about the isolation of the house echoed within her head, bringing with them a definite sense of uncertainty. Oh, for heaven's sake, that was exactly what he'd intended; to make her question whether she was doing the right thing; to make her change her mind over selling up.

3

Jazz eventually made the move to Cliff House, despite wondering right up to the last minute whether she was doing the right thing, and by early February was well and truly settled in. Even so, she couldn't help asking herself, what now? You can't stand around here all day — you need something to do —

That something quite often entailed standing in her favourite spot on the cliff top, gazing out over the sea, usually with a mug of coffee in her hand, which is precisely where she was on the afternoon that a man's voice startled her by calling, 'Jasmine?'

She whirled. She hadn't been called Jasmine in years. She'd long ago shortened it to Jazz. She watched as someone she didn't recognise strode across the grass towards her. For a second, she'd thought it was Zak Rivers come to repeat his offer to buy the house, although reason told her he wouldn't be calling her Jasmine. In fact, this man was several inches shorter than Zak, and nowhere near as intimidating. He was also grinning broadly, his blue eyes warm with delight at seeing her.

'You don't remember me, do you?' His smile wavered slightly as he went on, 'I'm mortified. I've never forgotten you.'

'Um — no, I'm sorry — ' She wrinkled her brow as he came nearer. She didn't recognise him — yet, there was something —

'Joel — ' he said. 'Joel Scott.'

'Joel!' The memories flooded back. He was a neighbour's son; she'd played with him although he'd been a year or two older than her. He'd been a kind, good-natured boy — well, for most of the time. 'I'm so sorry.' She held out a hand to take the one he'd stretched out to her.

'That's okay. I heard you were back.

47

It's been a long time.' He eyed her curiously. 'You suddenly stopped coming. I never did manage to discover why.'

She suspected that, like Zak Rivers, he was fishing for information. Were all the locals going to be this nosy? Well, she wasn't going to provide fodder for the gossips, so she didn't answer. In any case, what could she say? My parents wouldn't let me and like you I never discovered why. She couldn't, so she said nothing.

'I'm really sorry about Emily.' He didn't look offended by her lack of a response. 'We often bumped into each other in the town, had a chat. She was a lovely lady — '

'Thank you. It was a terrible shock — Do you still live next door?' If you could call it next door. Joel's house lay a good two, three hundred metres along the lane, towards the town.

'I do. Sadly, I lost both of my parents — a boating accident a few years back — and like you, decided to stay on in the house — ' He glanced over his shoulder at the house. 'Will you be okay here — all alone?'

What was it with these men? All so keen to point out the drawbacks of living alone. Did they really think she was so pathetic that she couldn't live without a man to turn to? 'I'm not sure yet. I'll work something out — I did think I might do a spot of B&B.'

'You've heard about the offer to buy it, I suppose?'

'Yes, Emily's solicitor initially told me. I've received two offers, actually.'

'I heard. Zak Rivers and, of course, I already knew about my boss's offer. He's Blake Carlisle.'

'Oh, you work for him. I haven't heard from him in person — '

'He owns several caravan parks all over the south west. He's always looking to expand. His motto is 'enough is never enough.' He'd convert the house to a couple of holiday apartments and erect ten or maybe twelve luxury chalets around it. We're planning to cater for wealthy clientele who prefer the privacy of their own accommodation rather than being stuck in a hotel. But you're not interested in selling, clearly, as you've moved in.'

'No, I'm not. Emily would have been appalled at the idea, and I have to admit, so am I. So — what do you do for Mr Carlisle?'

'I manage some of the caravan parks; you know — handle the rentals, bookings, any maintenance problems that arise — that sort of thing. I also visit the sites on a regular basis to keep an eye on things. I invested my inheritance in a couple of local parks and now part own them, so, you might say, I have a personal interest — '

'I see.'

'Yeah, Blake's an extremely astute business man. You ought to consider his offer if you get bored with it down here. Of course, I hope you won't.' Admiration gleamed as his glance slid over her. 'I hope we can get to know each other again.'

'I'd like that.'

And she would, she wasn't merely being polite. She'd liked Joel all those years ago when they were just children. It would also be reassuring to know he was just a little way along the lane, despite her resolve to be totally independent.

'And don't forget, I'm on hand if you should ever need anything. Don't hesitate to call — '

'Thank you, Joel. I'll keep that in mind.'

'Well, must go, lots to do. I thought I'd just call, let you know I'm still here.'

* * *

Once he'd gone, Jazz hurried back into the house. The afternoon had unexpectedly taken a turn for the worse. Banks of leaden cloud were building up, blotting out the blue of the sky, and a sharp wind was beginning to blow, transforming what had been a relatively calm sea into a grey maelstrom, sending waves crashing noisily against the rocks below, catapulting their foam high into the air as they did so. She had a feeling that she was about to experience her first stormy night since moving down here. She shivered as she walked, wrapping her arms tightly around herself, drawing comfort from the fact that she had a fire she could light. She'd do that right away, she promised herself, and draw the curtains — even though it wasn't yet dark — thereby shutting the storm out.

By the next morning, the storm had blown itself out and the day dawned bright and sunny once again. She'd lain in bed trying to sleep, nervously listening to the gale battering the walls of the building and the sound of the rain driving into the glass of the windows. Maybe Zak Rivers had been right. It was entirely different being here in the summer months to being here — alone — in the midst of winter. It didn't help that the house creaked and groaned as if it were alive. In the end, just as she'd done as a child, she'd covered her head with the quilt, closing everything out. So, it was a considerable relief the next morning to see the wintry sunshine slanting through a gap in the curtains and to hear the calling of the gulls as they swooped and wheeled above the roof.

She slipped her arms into her dressing gown and padded down the stairs to the kitchen. The Aga that Emily had installed ensured that the room was always warm. She made some tea and, dragging a stool across, took refuge alongside it, fingers wrapped around her mug, as she made plans for the rest of the day.

She decided to pay a visit to Beth Goodwin, Emily's friend who had initially phoned her with the news of her aunt's death. She hadn't had the opportunity to speak to her at any length at the funeral and there were several questions she wanted to ask. She'd discovered her address by consulting the phone directory, so a visit would be her first task of the day. It was time she got to know a few of the locals — nosy or not — otherwise she was going to be very lonely. She might even get in one or two questions about Zak Rivers.

She dressed in jeans and a thick sweater, and then pulled on a warm, fleece-lined jacket. It was quite a walk to Beth's house — maybe she should phone first? A woman's voice responded after the first ring. She was going to be at home and she said she'd love to see Jazz. 'Come straight along,' she warmly invited, 'I'll put the coffee pot on — '

A brisk walk along the high-hedged lane that led to the town cleared Jazz's head of the few remaining dregs of sleep. The air was crisp and cold, the sky an unbroken blue, a complete contrast to the night before. She passed Joel's house and paused for a moment; it looked deserted so she didn't linger.

By the time she reached Beth's small, terraced house, she was out of breath.

The land that surrounded the town climbed steeply, and although it had all been downhill all the way for Jazz, her legs ached. The town itself nestled in a hollow, fronted by the estuary and a harbour that eventually opened out into the sea. Beth's house was on the opposite side of the town to where Cliff House stood, at the very end of the main street, Fore Street, at the point where the road began to climb once more. Jazz was pleased to note, that unlike a lot of holiday towns, St. Kernan still possessed shops that catered to the residents' everyday needs.

She didn't linger, though, and was soon knocking upon the door of number forty two. It was flung open almost at once and there was Beth, a short, plump woman, her smile a warmly welcoming one.

'Jazz.' She made a grab for Jazz's hand and proceeded to energetically shake it. 'It's so good to meet you properly at last. I've heard such a lot about you over the past years. Your aunt was terribly fond of you — Come in, dear; please, come in — '

Jazz followed her into a cosy kitchen.

'I thought we'd sit in here, it's the warmest room in the house. Now — I've got the coffee all ready.'

There was no hint of reproach for Jazz not having visited Emily for the past sixteen or so years, and it suddenly occurred to her that perhaps Beth would know the truth of what had happened between her mother and her only sister.

Within moments, they were sitting, holding mugs of strong, fragrant coffee.

'Now,' Beth smiled at her, 'what did you want to talk about?'

'My aunt and what happened at the end. I mean — ' Jazz took a cautious sip of the scalding coffee, 'I can't believe there were there no warning signs of a heart problem.'

'Well, in the last week or so she did complain of tiredness — which wasn't like her. She'd always been so full of energy, go — but she just put it down to getting older. Of course, now I realise she should have gone to see her doctor — but how were we to know?' Her eyes glistened with tears.

'Please — don't upset yourself.' Jazz bent over the table at which they were sitting and patted the older woman's hand. 'It's me that should feel guilty — for not coming — I made the terrible mistake of believing that there was time, time to come and see her again — '

'Nothing is certain in this world, my dear. But I know exactly what you mean — we think things will go on the same way, that we'll have infinite time to put things right, to make amends.'

'D-did Emily ever explain what happened between her and my mother? Say why I hadn't been to visit? Why I hadn't been allowed — ?' Jazz's voice broke. 'Presumably she must have mentioned the rift — if she spoke about me?'

Beth shook her head. 'She did say

there'd been some sort of argument — years ago, and you'd been stopped from coming here. I know it broke her heart. That was when she really threw herself into developing her business. She worked all hours God sent. I used to say to her — Em, you'll kill yourself at this rate — ' her expression darkened, ' — and just look — that's exactly what happened. But,' she shook her head, 'she wouldn't listen.' She smiled then at Jazz. 'She was always so pleased whenever you wrote to her or phoned. She'd ring me straight away, relate word for word what you'd said — or written. Oh dear me — ' she wiped her eyes, 'just look at me — silly old fool that I am, but — ' her voice broke, ' — I miss her so much.' She seemed to almost shake herself then. 'Of course, I didn't know her when you used to come. I moved here just afterwards. But, make no mistake, she loved you dearly.'

Jazz nodded, her own tears springing

up. 'I should have visited — as I got older. But — it would have felt like a betrayal of my mother. I should have come though,' she repeated. 'She never uttered a single word of reproach.'

Beth stretched out a hand again. 'She knew you loved her. That's why she left you her house. She'd always been so happy there. She wanted you to be the same. She'd be so pleased that you've come to stay.'

'Was . . . was she alone when she died?'

'Sadly, yes.'

'Who found her?'

'I did. We were supposed to be going out for the evening. I'd managed to persuade her to give the accounts a rest, she would insist on doing the books on a daily basis — We were both alone, you see. My husband left me a few years ago — Anyway, a new restaurant had opened nearby and we were going to give it a try. I had a key, so when she didn't answer the ring of the doorbell, I went in — ' She brushed a hand across her eyes. 'Oh my, what a shock — what a dreadful, dreadful shock — She was sitting there in the armchair, all dressed ready to go — ' She fell silent for a moment, as if the memory of that terrible evening was simply too painful to talk about. 'She looked — frightened, I suppose. Maybe she'd known what was happening — ?' She shook her head. 'I'll never forget it, never.'

They both sat in silence, pondering events, the finality of death — the awful fragility of life. It was Jazz who eventually spoke again. 'You probably know I've had a couple of offers to buy Cliff House.'

'Yes — one of them from Zak Rivers I believe?'

Jazz was relieved to see Beth's sadness lift. She nodded. 'I found him in my garden the morning after I'd been to see the solicitor.'

'That sounds like Zak Rivers. Never one to hang about once he's decided on a course of action. It's what's made him such a successful business man, I suppose — '

'Do you know him?'

'Oh, yes, everyone knows everyone else in St. Kernan. Of course, I wouldn't describe him as a friend — as such, but we speak whenever we pass each other in the street. He's always very pleasant, but apart from that, I don't really know much about him.'

'Would you tell me what you do know?'

The older woman seemed only too eager to confide. In fact, she spoke with undisguised relish. 'Well, rumour has it he's very rich, self made, clever, quite ruthless, by all accounts, with fingers in all sorts of pies, from property and holiday parks, to engineering and DIY shops. He did inherit some money from his grandfather, I believe, which he's turned into several million — but as I said, that's just gossip, really. He lives in the Old Manor House, amongst acres and acres of parkland. He values his

privacy. Trespassers are always pros-
ecuted — so I've heard. He's got no
time for fools.'

For someone who professed to not
know much about him, Beth was
coming out with a great deal of detail.
'Married?'

'No, but from what I've heard, he's
had dozens of girlfriends over the years.
'Course he'd be quite a catch for some
woman.'

'I s'pose. A touch — no, I'll rephrase
that — very arrogant, I thought. I'll
make an educated guess that he
invariably gets what he wants.'

'Aah, so you do know a bit about
him. It's amazing what money will buy.'

'Well, it's not buying Cliff House.'

'Good for you. He'd made Emily an
offer too, you know, not that long
before she died.'

He hadn't mentioned that. 'How long
before?'

'Oh, let me see — two, maybe three
months. She turned him down of
course. Emily would never have sold

Cliff House.' Beth eyed her. 'You haven't said who the other offer was from.'

'Someone called Carlisle, Blake Carlisle.'

Beth didn't seem surprised. 'Oh yes. Now I think about it, Emily mentioned him. But he hadn't sounded that keen — accepted her refusal with no argument. Whereas Zak Rivers — '

'Yes?'

'Well, he seemed keener, said he'd top anyone else's offer.'

'Yes,' Jazz murmured, 'he said the same to me.'

'Maybe he'd heard Carlisle was interested and wanted to pip him to the post. I think there's a bit of rivalry goes on there — Well, that's natural I suppose, them being in the same sort of business, so to speak. Have you met Carlisle's assistant, Joel somebody or other?' She clucked her tongue with annoyance at herself. 'Of course, you must have. He lives right next door to you.'

'I used to play with him when I came here as a child. He was a bit older than me, but we got on okay. He was a kind boy, took care of me. He called in too — just to let me know he was still around. He lives alone, so — I presume he hasn't married? I didn't like to ask.'

'No, although he's had a few girlfriends too, I believe. Have you met his boss?'

'No, I've been expecting him to get in touch. What's he like?'

'Nothing special, he made his money in caravan parks. He lives out on the Truro road with his wife and son in a huge house; swimming pool, gym — the lot. Like something out of Dallas — I can't imagine how he got planning permission.' She sniffed disparagingly. 'Still, they say — money talks, don't they? In my opinion, he's all show and very little taste, although I've heard he's got his head screwed on.'

'Yes, Joel said that.'

Jazz was thoughtful as she headed back home. She'd learnt a lot from

Beth — especially about Emily. Her aunt had clearly had a fulfilling life, even if she worked too hard.

But there had been one thing that had disturbed her in all that Beth had said. She'd thought Emily had looked frightened. Why? What could have frightened her — the thought of death? Had she known she was dying as Beth had wondered? If so, then why hadn't she called for help? No time? Could it really have happened that fast?

4

It was that evening that Jazz first heard what sounded like footsteps in one of the bedrooms. She didn't pay much attention at first, simply glancing up from her newspaper, then, when it all fell silent again, she carried on reading, deciding the sounds had merely been the creaking of old floorboards. When it happened once more at exactly the same time the next evening, she began to feel nervous. It did sound exactly like someone walking across the bedroom floor. The third evening that she heard it she nerved herself to go upstairs to check it out. To her relief, there was no-one and nothing there. When it didn't happen again, she put the whole thing down to the sounds of ancient timbers expanding or contracting, and dismissed it from her mind.

She'd seen nothing more of either

Zak Rivers or Joel, so she'd also put them and their offers to buy Cliff House out of her head. That was until Joel turned up on her doorstep one evening a fortnight after she'd first moved in, bearing a huge bouquet of flowers, mainly the heavily perfumed white lilies, as well as a bottle of champagne.

'I've been very remiss,' he grinned, 'in not welcoming you properly as a neighbour. So, here I am. Shall we open this and make an evening of it?' and he waved the bottle at her.

Jazz's heart lifted to see him. She'd been having a fit of the blues, wondering, for the umpteenth time, whether she'd made a terrible mistake in moving down here, away from all of her friends; away from her job. 'That would be great.'

She hurried into the kitchen to find some glasses. She knew Emily had champagne flutes somewhere. She just couldn't remember where she'd seen them. She opened one cupboard door after another, until she discovered them at the very back of the last one she tried. She lifted them out and with a dramatic 'Da-da' held them out to Joel.

'Cheers,' he said, as they both took their first mouthfuls, 'here's to a long and happy life in St. Kernan.'

It wasn't until they were seated on either side of the fire that, despite having dismissed it all from her mind, Jazz heard herself asking, 'Did Emily ever mention hearing anything — here, in the house?'

Joel frowned at her. 'Hearing anything? What like? What do you mean?'

'It sounded like footsteps.' Oh Lord. He was going to think she'd lost her mind.

'What! You've heard footsteps? Are you sure?' And suddenly he was the boy that she remembered from sixteen years ago, eyes glittering, lips parted, eager to hear more. It was just the sort of question that would have inspired him to imagine all kinds of weird and wonderful things.

'We-ell, I was probably imagining things — '

'Tell me everything,' he demanded. 'Where did you hear them?'

'I heard — or thought I heard — something — in the bedroom above here — on three consecutive evenings. Only for a few moments, but — '

'It scared you?'

'Well, not scared exactly, more — made me nervous, I suppose. I went up to have a look,' she gave a snort of laughter, 'of course, there was no-one there. It was probably the floorboards expanding or something. I'm just not used to old houses — '

'Emily did mention once that the house seemed to be creaking a lot more — a bit like her, she said. There was a sort of tension about her over the last few weeks — she looked worn down — ' He eyed her, the glitter of excitement replaced now by what looked like anxiety. 'Maybe I shouldn't have told you that. But I wondered if something was worrying her.'

The doorbell rang, startling them both, so much so, that they both jumped, Jazz spilling some of her champagne in the process. It landed in her lap, leaving a fairly large wet patch. 'Who can that be?'

She stood up and, glass in hand, went to open the door. Zak Rivers was standing there, the last person she'd expected to see. He too was holding a bottle; not a bottle of champagne, his offering was a very good red wine.

'Ah,' he said with a rueful grin, 'I can see I'm too late. Never mind, you can keep this for some other time — ' It was as if their initial, barbed exchange had never happened. He was behaving as a friend would, and he was far from that.

'Who is it?' Joel called, sticking his head out around the door leading from the sitting room. 'What the hell are you doing here, Rivers?'

Zak didn't bother responding to that. So Jazz, rather reluctantly, stepped into the breach. 'Um — Mr Rivers and I met on my first visit to St. Kernan.

Won't you come in?'

'Please, call me Zak.'

As she had the first time he'd made it, Jazz disregarded the overture. She only called people she knew well by their Christian names, and, as yet, she barely knew this man at all. 'Um, will you have a glass of champagne with us?' There seemed nothing else to do but invite him to join them. 'Joel very kindly brought it — as a gesture of welcome to me.'

'Thank you — no. I'm not a lover of champagne. If you have a corkscrew, though, I'll have a glass of this — ' and he indicated the bottle of wine. Claret if Jazz wasn't mistaken. In truth, she too would have preferred wine to champagne. She went to the kitchen and returned with a corkscrew and a wineglass.

'Well, I'm sure there's no need for an introduction,' she brightly said. They clearly didn't like each other. Not surprisingly, she supposed, if they were business rivals.

'No,' they simultaneously and abruptly said.

'We know each other, of course,' Joel said. 'So — I suppose you've come with another offer, Rivers?'

'I could assume the same of you,' Zak curtly riposted.

'I'm here, as Jazz said, to welcome a new neighbour. But as Jazz is hardly a neighbour of yours — '

'I regard all the townspeople as neighbours,' Zak smoothly said. 'St. Kernan is only a small place, after all.'

When Joel didn't respond to that, Zak bent his attention to the deft removal of the cork from the bottle of wine. Jazz handed him the glass. He smiled his thanks, his glance moving over her, missing nothing, she was sure, not even the damp patch on her jeans.

'So — ' he said, 'how are you settling in?'

'Very well, thank you. Getting used to all the different noises — '

She bit her lip. She hadn't meant to say that. It would sound as if she was confirming his presumption that she'd be nervous living here alone. 'You know — the creaks of floorboards, etcetera. It's all new to me — obviously.'

'Quite. And then there's the sound of the sea so close, the howl of the wind, not to mention the horizontal rain slamming against the windows — '

'Yes, all that too, but none of it bothers me — ' she airily and mendaciously assured him.

Zak drained his glass. 'That's good to hear. Well, I won't stay — as you've already got company.' His expression was a serious one suddenly. 'You won't forget what I said the last time we met, will you?'

Joel's ears almost physically twitched at that. Jazz hid a smile. Zak was referring to his offer to outbid any other interested party in Cliff House. 'No, but don't hold your breath.'

'How can I help it when you're around?' And he grinned provocatively at her.

It was at that moment that she

understood what women would see in him, and, to her horror, felt herself blushing, which, of course, only intensified the gleam in his eye. Damn, damn. Now, he'd think she was affected by his words, by him; flattered, even. The very last impression she wanted to give.

'I'll see you out — ' she hurriedly said.

'No, please — stay with your — guest.' He placed, what Jazz considered, an unnecessary emphasis on the word. Why? Was it to imply that Joel had insinuated his way into the house with some sort of ulterior motive, that he wasn't there solely as a guest? As possibly Zak himself had? Jazz experienced a surge of irritation. Really! Who did he think he was? And what was it to do with him anyway who she invited into her home? 'I know the way out.'

'I'll bet he does,' Joel muttered once Zak had gone.

'What do you mean?' She was becoming a tad exasperated with this overt display of — what — testosterone;

machismo? They seemed to be vying with each other for her attention — like two boys arguing over a toy.

'Well, it was a conversation I overheard between him and your aunt in the White Swan pub one evening.'

'Yes? Go on — ' The White Swan was the nearest pub to Cliff House. She'd had no idea that Emily frequented it.

'Rivers seemed to be — well, talking rather earnestly about something; pressing her, almost. I couldn't actually hear what he was saying — I'd also seen his car parked outside here a couple of times, so he'd obviously been to see her.'

'He had made her an offer for Cliff House, Beth told me. She didn't mention him putting pressure on her, though — ' She gazed at him thoughtfully. 'Did my aunt ever mention to you that he was pressing her over anything?'

'Well, no — ' he smiled weakly, 'but she does — did lease her shop from him, and she did mention to me that the lease would soon be due for renewal. We were talking in the shop one day. I'd gone in to ask her to quote for some new curtains — But I wonder now — if in his eagerness to secure this place, well — supposing he was refusing to renew the lease if she didn't sell Cliff House to him? She often looked worn down, worried almost — as I said — in those final weeks.'

Jazz frowned. 'But you have no proof that that's what he was doing?'

Joel shook his head. 'No, but — '

'Would he do something like that?' She mutely scoffed at her naïvety. Of course he would. She was quite sure he'd do whatever it took to acquire whatever it was he wanted. She'd decided that on their first encounter.

And Joel appeared to agree with her. 'Huh! Who knows what Rivers would be capable of? He wants this house and he didn't get where he is today by being soft hearted, and I won't deny I have wondered, what with Emily looking anxious.'

A deep sense of misgiving was starting within Jazz.

'In fact, I have wondered since whether the worry of maybe losing her shop if he wouldn't renew the lease could, in some way, have contributed to her heart attack. You know — brought it on — '

★ ★ ★

That night, instead of falling asleep the minute her head touched the pillow as she usually did, Jazz tossed and turned as Joel's disturbing words echoed ceaselessly in her head. Was he right? Had Zak been pressuring Emily to sell by threatening not to renew her shop lease unless she sold him her house? Was he really capable of something like that? And, if he was, then, as Joel had suggested, could the fear of losing her precious shop, have led directly to her death? Beth had told Jazz Emily had looked frightened when she found her.

Something else occurred to her then. Could Zak have physically threatened her? She recalled her own feelings of intimidation, of menace, at their first encounter — had that been how Emily had felt?

This was no good. The questions were going round and round in her head. She climbed out of bed and went down to the kitchen where she made herself a large mug of cocoa, hoping it would make her drowsy enough to sleep. So, she was fully awake, in the sitting room, staring into the dying embers of the fire, when she heard the sounds for the fourth time: unmistakable footsteps — crossing the floor above her. She sat, staring up at the ceiling, as if that would reveal who or what was up there.

And it was then that a truly horrifying question presented itself to her. Could her aunt have been hearing the same thing? Could it have so frightened her — ? Oh God! Could this have been what she was hearing right before she died? If Zak was so desperate to buy Cliff House, could he possibly have something to do with it? Rather than refuse the renewal of her lease, could he have made some sort of cruel attempt to scare her into selling to him that had backfired and instead scared her to death? And was he trying to do the same to Jazz? After all, he'd already tried to frighten her by emphasising the perils of living alone in such an isolated house. But — how on earth would he manage to get into the house? He'd have to break and enter and when she'd checked before, there'd been no sign of forced entry or of anyone having been in the bedroom.

She put down her mug of cocoa and walked into the hallway. She listened intently, but could hear nothing. There was no sound out here. Right, if this was some callous, cruel trick, then she'd do her utmost to expose it. Expose Zak Rivers for the scoundrel he was.

She mounted the stairs two at a time, and flung open the bedroom door. Just as before, the room was undisturbed; no-one was there. Had she really expected there to be? Even so, determined to check everything, she slowly circled the room; she even opened the wardrobe door once again and looked inside, knowing she was being foolish but quite unable to help herself. If it was Zak, he'd hardly be hiding inside, would he? Waiting for her to discover him?

She turned her gaze to the window, which was securely latched with the curtains undrawn. She peered through, but saw only the empty garden. It was a windy night; the powerful gusts rattled the windows in their frames, and slammed into the walls of the house. She shivered and hugged herself tightly as she turned to leave the room. A floorboard creaked noisily beneath her feet. There — relief flooded through her — there was the only possible explanation, just as she'd initially thought. It was nothing more sinister than creaking timbers. It didn't occur to her that the floor hadn't creaked until she'd walked upon it.

5

Beth rang the next morning and issued an invitation that, for a short while, drove all else from Jazz's mind.

'I'm going to have a party,' she announced, 'cold buffet, gallons of cheap plonk, informal, friendly, to introduce you to some of the local people. We all need cheering up at this time of year and I know Emily would approve. She'd want you to meet everyone, to feel at home. I've got several friends you'd like. There's one in particular, Julie. She's about your age.'

'Oh, Beth, that sounds wonderful.'

And it did. It could be just what she needed. She'd come to the conclusion that she was spending too much time alone with only her thoughts for company. It was people she needed; friends, in fact.

'Good. It will be all very low key as I've said. Now — will Saturday suit you? Eight o'clock?'

⋆　⋆　⋆

And, as if the heavens approved of Beth's plan, Saturday dawned bright and sunny, the temperature the highest it had been since Jazz had arrived in St. Kernan. The sea, a vivid aquamarine beneath the cloudless sky, lapped gently at the rocks, and the harbour was so calm it resembled the proverbial mill pond. It could have been a summer's day. This was how she remembered it from her long ago holidays. Emily would have bounced into her room crying, 'Come on, lazybones. We'll take a picnic to the beach and look for crabs.'

She smiled fondly at the memory and went down to the kitchen. She'd heard no further noises of any sort and resolved to put all of the previous incidents out of her mind. She was allowing her imagination to get the better of her and it had to stop. With that in mind, she took her breakfast out onto the small terrace that overlooked the sea and passed the time by wondering who would be at the party. Someone interesting, she hoped. Maybe she should involve herself in local affairs — if she could discover what was going on? There were bound to be associations; clubs, even. Maybe she could take an evening class at the nearby college? She'd get herself a prospectus — Her spirit lifted. Maybe she'd even get a job? Find something a bit more interesting than what she'd been doing previously; something that would provide a challenge. She was computer literate so the world could be her oyster. She'd put out a few feelers this evening, depending on who was at Beth's, of course.

By seven thirty she was brimming with optimism and a fair amount of excitement at the thought of what the evening might have in store for her.

Naturally, she wanted to look her best, so she opted for her favourite pair of silky black trousers and a green top which did amazing things for her eyes. A V-shaped neckline revealed the beginnings of her high breasts.

The town was a little too far to walk to at night so she went in her car, hoping she'd be able to park somewhere close to Beth's house. St. Kernan wasn't awash with car parks but there were a few spaces on a nearby quay. She was in luck and found a vacant spot. She was also the first to arrive.

'Sorry, Beth,' she returned Beth's warm smile of greeting, 'am I too early?'

'No, the others are late. Come on in. I've got some mulled wine all ready — '

Beth all but dragged her into the kitchen where a table was practically overflowing with food. 'How many are coming?'

'Oh, about thirty or so — '

'Thirty!' Jazz had been expecting a dozen or so. She glanced round the small kitchen. How on earth would Beth fit thirty people in?

Beth seemed unconcerned, however. 'Yes. The more the merrier, I always say — I think a good crowd makes a better atmosphere.'

'Beth — I know Emily told you that Zak Rivers offered to buy Cliff House — ' she paused, wondering, for a second, whether to go on or not, ' — did she ever mention anything about him putting pressure on her to sell the house? Or that he threatened not to renew the lease on the shop if she wouldn't agree?'

'Good heavens, no.' Beth appeared shocked. 'Mind you, she didn't talk about the shop that much — probably knew I wouldn't understand the mechanics of it. I'm a bit clueless about any sort of business — Why, I didn't even know the lease was up for renewal. But — why would you ask such a thing?'

'Well — I've heard she looked anxious, stressed, even — before she died. And his car had been seen outside the house — plus, he was heard — well, pressing her about something in the White Swan one evening.'

'Pressing her — what about?'

'Well, that's the trouble. I don't know.'

Beth was beginning to look worried. 'She did look tired — as I told you, but anxious or worried — I didn't notice if she did and I'm sure I would have. Although, I suppose tiredness could look like anxiety to some people — Oh dear, you've got me worried now — Who told you all of this?'

'Joel.'

'Well, if anything like that was happening, she certainly didn't tell me.'

'I'm sure it was nothing then.'

Beth nodded her agreement, just as the doorbell chimed, heralding the first of the evening's guests. Within half an hour, Beth's small house was crammed with people, and by the time Jazz had been introduced to everyone, she'd been invited to join the carnival committee and persuaded to help out in the lifeboat shop. Julie, as Beth had promised, was her age, twenty four, pretty and very friendly, and, apart from Jazz, the youngest there.

'You'll have to join me and my friends for an evening out — '

'I'd love to.'

Jazz saw Joel come in, and make a beeline for her.

'Hi,' he said, 'I see you've met Julie — hi, Julie.' The young woman blushed and pouted prettily. She obviously liked Joel, Jazz decided. Mind you, he was a very attractive young man. But Joel didn't seem to return her sentiment. He certainly wasn't paying her any attention. Instead, his glance was wandering round the room, looking for something — or someone. 'Good crowd here. It was kind of Mrs Goodwin to invite me.'

'Beth's like that — '

Joel looked around again. 'I can't see Rivers.'

Ah, that's who he was looking for. Jazz knew Beth had invited Zak, but she hadn't actually said whether he was coming or not. She hoped if he did turn up; there wouldn't be any sort of argument between the two men.

'Oh Lord, why didn't I keep my mouth shut?' Joel groaned then. 'Talk of the devil and he's bound to appear.'

Jazz followed Joel's gaze and, sure enough, there stood Zak Rivers. He was in the process of greeting Beth, and waving to a couple of other people when he saw Jazz — and then Joel.

'What's the betting he comes over?' Joel muttered. 'If he starts to try and persuade you to sell — '

'Surely he won't do that, not here?' Jazz murmured.

'Huh! You clearly don't know Zak Rivers very well then if you think that.'

Joel, however, was proved wrong. Zak didn't join them. In fact, he attached himself to a small group on the far side of the room — as distant from Jazz and Joel as he could physically get. Jazz felt slighted; ignored — which was totally irrational as he was the last person she wanted to have to talk to. Obviously he only wanted to know her if she was prepared to accept his offer to buy her house. Well, that wasn't about to happen so she doubted that she'd have any further contact with him.

'Don't blame you for looking in that direction — ' Julie whispered; she'd obviously noticed Jazz's glances at Zak. 'Good looks — if you like the rugged sort — which I have to admit I do — money — every girl's dream, really. Have you met him yet?' Before Jazz could say yes, Julie was literally dragging her over to where Zak was talking intently to another man.

'Oh, please, Julie — no, I'd rather not — '

'Don't be silly. He's come especially to meet you — Mr Rivers,' Julie called as they neared him, 'have you met our newest resident?'

'Julie, please — ' Jazz pleaded, hideously embarrassed. Zak couldn't have made it plainer he wasn't interested in talking to her.

But, contrary to her expectation of a cool snub, Zak swung to face them both, a smile lifting his lips. 'Yes, I've had that pleasure — twice now.' His glance shifted from Jazz's slightly pink face to Julie. 'And you are?'

Jazz was surprised. From Julie's manner, she'd thought she knew Zak. 'Julie Barlow. I live not far from you, actually I see you quite often — passing in your car — ' Julie was valiantly trying to hide her wounded feelings. Evidently, she'd expected that Zak would have known her, or at least recognised her as a neighbour. 'I'm a great admirer of your house,' she went on, clearly intent on disregarding the slight, 'it must be amazing inside.'

'Well, I like it. You'll have to come and see it sometime — '

Jazz heard Julie's gasp of ecstatic surprise. Zak did too — judging by his broadening grin. 'Bring Jazz with you.'

'Oh, I will — um, we will, won't we, Jazz?'

Jazz, for her part, was mortified. If

ever anyone had been forced into issuing an invitation, Zak had been. 'Oh — well, I don't think — ' Jazz stammered.

'Oh, come on, Jazz,' Zak quietly urged. 'It'll give you some idea of how I do things. I organised the renovations myself.'

Julie was staring — almost pleadingly — at Jazz. Jazz smiled weakly. 'Zak — um, Mr Rivers — '

'Zak will do,' he quietly put in, 'as I keep telling you.'

This time, she complied with his request. 'Zak wants to buy Cliff House and convert it into a luxury hotel,' she told Julie.

'Wow!' Julie's eyes were even wider by this time.

'But I'm not interested in selling.'

Zak shrugged at that, as if the matter were of little or no concern to him, when, if Joel were to be believed, it was the exact opposite.

As a result of this — pretence in Jazz's view, her next remark was a curt one. 'And neither was my aunt, apparently.'

'Quite, and I readily accepted her refusal.'

'That's not what I heard — ' Jazz blurted, only to immediately regret it when she saw the way in which Zak's glance sharpened; narrowed.

'Oh, really, and what did you hear — exactly?' He was watching her now from beneath heavy eyelids. All trace of mirth had fled.

'Um — ' Jazz felt completely wrong-footed. Even Joel hadn't known for sure whether Zak had been talking to Emily about buying the house when he'd seen them together; he'd just put two and two together — knowing that Zak wanted Cliff House. ' — that you were — um, were trying to persuade her — '

'And who did you hear that from, I wonder? No, don't tell me. Let me guess — Scott?' His tone was one of utter contempt. 'You really shouldn't believe all that you hear, Jazz.'

'So — you weren't trying to persuade her?'

But she wasn't to get an answer to that, because Zak had already turned away as a woman came up behind him and linked her arm affectionately with his. 'Sara,' he said, with transparent pleasure, 'how lovely to see you.' He did turn back to Jazz and Julie then, to say, 'Will you excuse me?' before moving away with the newcomer.

'Wow! Who is that?' Julie softly asked. 'She's gorgeous — '

'Haven't a clue, but she seems to know Zak extremely well.'

And she was very beautiful. Could she be a girlfriend? Yet, he hadn't greeted her like that. As if on cue, Beth arrived, holding a large platter of finger food. Beth would be sure to know who she was — she'd ask her.

'Here you are, girls, help your-selves — '

'Who's that with Zak?' Julie had done it for her. A tiny pang of relief pierced

Jazz. It was much better coming from Julie.

'Oh, that's Sara Gresham. A daughter of a good friend of mine, her mother's here somewhere. Sara and Zak went out together for a while — '

Well, that would explain the warmth of Zak's greeting. What it didn't explain was her feeling of — chagrin; disappointment? Although why that should be she couldn't have said. She didn't give a damn what Zak Rivers did or didn't do.

She went to fetch herself another drink, a soft one this time as she had to drive home. Joel was also at the drinks table, helping himself to a whisky. He looked distinctly displeased.

'I thought you'd deserted me, going off like that with Julie — '

'Sorry. Julie thought I hadn't been introduced to Zak, when in reality,' she grinned, trying to lighten Joel's dark mood, 'it was her that wanted to meet him.'

'Hmm.' He didn't look mollified by

this explanation. Instead, he continued to glower in Zak's direction. 'I see one of his old flames has turned up.'

'Oh — do you know her?'

'Hardly,' he snorted disparagingly. 'I don't move in her exalted circles. She has some sort of high flying job in Truro — She certainly wouldn't look — even once — at me. I'm much too commonplace. And I certainly don't have enough money. Rivers is much more her cup of tea.'

'Who's he seeing at the moment?' she casually asked.

'Haven't a clue. Why? You're not interested, are you?' His glance at her was a piercing one.

'Me?' she scoffed. 'What a ridiculous notion. No.'

'Maybe it's him that's interested in you. Had you thought about that?'

'Well, only in as far as he wants my house.'

'Yes and courting you could be one way of getting his hands on it.'

'Don't be silly,' she snorted, 'not even

Zak Rivers would go that far — '

'Zak Rivers wouldn't go how far?'

Jazz gasped and whirled, only to discover Zak standing right behind them.

6

Oh-my-God! Jazz agonised. How much of their conversation had he heard?

'We were talking about you, not to you, Rivers.' Joel didn't look the least put out by Zak's sudden appearance — unlike Jazz, who was staring, horrified, at Zak.

'Re-really, it-it was nothing,' she finally managed to stammer. 'Sorry.' After which, the only thing she could think to do was to make a very hasty escape.

Not surprisingly, from that moment the party lost its appeal for Jazz, and she was soon pleading tiredness to Beth in preparation for a second fast escape. 'Sorry, Beth, it's been wonderful, but I haven't had much sleep for the past few nights — too many creaking floorboards; too much to think about.'

Zak's voice came once more from

behind her. The wretched man had done it again, crept up behind her. Was it deliberate? Was he hoping he would hear something he could use to better his chances of buying Cliff House? 'Now — if you moved into a nice new house, you wouldn't have that problem — '

'What problem?' she snapped.

'Creaky floorboards — that house is far too isolated for a woman living on her own.'

'So you keep telling me. But that's exactly why I like it, and why I won't be selling it. Goodnight, Mr Rivers — '

He sighed wearily. 'Oh dear, we're back to Mr Rivers again, are we?'

'We are.'

His gaze narrowed. 'How are you getting home?'

'The same way I came — in my car.'

'Would you like me to follow you, make sure you're okay?'

'Certainly not,' she bit out. Good grief, why did he think she'd need him? She was perfectly capable of looking after herself; she'd been doing it for years, after all.

But he wasn't to be fobbed off. 'It's very stormy and for someone who's unaccustomed to our Cornish winters.'

'I'll be fine.'

'I promise not to try and court you — if that's what you're worried about. Or, even worse, make love to you.'

There was a peculiar glitter to his eyes now. She couldn't decide whether it was anger or amusement. But one thing was embarrassingly evident; he had heard what she and Joel had said. This was getting worse by the second. She could kill Joel for his indiscretion. He must have known there was a risk he'd be overheard.

'I'm going that way, Rivers — obviously.' It was Joel. It must be his turn to eavesdrop? Really, she didn't know which one of them was the worst.

Zak held up both hands in a mute gesture of surrender. 'I'll say goodnight then.'

As Jazz walked to her car, she

wondered what had happened to his ex-girlfriend, Sara — wasn't it? Surely he'd want to see her home?

'I'll be right behind you,' Joel called as she battled her way through what felt like a force ten gale and almost horizontal rain to reach her car. Zak Rivers had been right about one thing, the weather.

It took only moments to reach Cliff House, despite the driving rain that made visibility almost non-existent. There were no street lights this far out of the town, and the darkness was absolute and impenetrable. She had expected Joel to turn into his own driveway, so she was surprised when she saw his headlights still behind her. She pulled into her own drive, opened the door and climbed out, only to be practically lifted her off her feet by the wind.

'Come on,' Joel shouted, making a grab for her, 'I'll help you inside.'

Jazz put her head down as they headed for the front door. She couldn't believe the change from the earlier blue skies and warm sunshine. But that was the English climate for you. So fickle it could change in a second.

She fumbled with the door key, all the time getting wetter and wetter.

'Here — let me,' Joel shouted through the howling of the wind. 'Emily said it could be a bit tricky at times — '

He took the key off her and almost at once had the door open. As one, they dived inside, to stand, dripping small puddles all over the hall floor.

'You'd better have a nightcap before you brave all that again.' Zak had been right — irritatingly so. It did feel better to have someone come in with her, even Joel, whom she was still annoyed with. She shivered, wrapping her arms about herself, as she made her way into the kitchen. Joel followed close behind.

'I hope it's warm in there,' he said, 'because I'm soaked through and freezing.'

Once they were standing before the Aga, he removed his coat and flung it onto the floor. Jazz retrieved it and draped it over one of the stools to dry in the heat. It began to gently steam.

'Okay. Hot drink or a whisky?' she asked.

'Ooh — hot drink, I think, seeing as how I have to venture back out into that grim night.'

Jazz made hot chocolate and they sat, perched on two more stools, drinking it and basking in the warmth.

'This is nice,' Joel said, 'quite like the old days. I recall us getting just as wet one afternoon — I think it had unexpectedly poured with rain — and your aunt made us the very same drink: hot chocolate.'

A vague memory of that came to Jazz. She smiled at the thought of Emily bustling round the kitchen. She missed her so much. If only — But she stopped her thoughts there. It was too late for regrets. All she could do for Emily now was to hang on to her beloved house. Emily would never have agreed to sell it; she knew that as surely as if her aunt were standing in the kitchen telling her so.

The rain slashed against the window as the wind screamed and howled. The very walls of the house seemed to shake. Jazz shivered again, despite the warmth radiating from the Aga.

'So,' Joel said, 'you're definitely staying here then?'

'Yes. I love it — all of it, even on a night like this: the house; the garden; being able to stand and look directly out to sea.'

'Well, if you can stand it at this time of the year, you should certainly be able to weather the summer time. Mind you,' he grimaced, 'what with all the visitors that descend upon us, I sometimes think these months are the best ones.'

'Ye-es, it might be a bit hectic; different. I was only ever here for three or four weeks at the most.'

'Well,' Joel gazed at her over the rim of his mug, 'if you should change your mind, Blake would always give you a decent sum for the house.'

'I've been thinking about all that — you know, yours and Zak's plans — '

For a split second, Joel's expression was a watchful one; guarded, even. 'Yes?'

'Well, what about permission, you know — to change the usage from a private dwelling to a caravan park? Would you get consent for that?'

Joel grinned, tapping the side of his nose knowingly. 'All settled.'

'Ah, I see.' That could only mean one thing: a bit of bribery and corruption. She studied him then. It would suit Joel, every bit as much as Zak and Blake, to buy the house and expand the business interests of South Western Enterprises if, as he said he had, he'd invested in a couple of the parks. 'And Zak Rivers — has he done the same?'

'I should imagine he's got it sorted.'

Yes, so would she. She couldn't imagine him wasting time and effort trying to buy a property if he hadn't already ensured he'd get planning permission to convert. It was beginning to look as if everyone had everyone else in their pockets. Not a comforting thought. Especially as the only thing to stand in the way of them getting what they wanted was her.

'Anyway,' Joel got to his feet, 'it sounds as if the rain's easing so I'll get off.'

'Okay. Thank you, Joel. It was reassuring to know that you were right behind me on the way back.'

'Any time; any time at all. I'm just at the end of the phone line.'

He retrieved his coat from the stool. It was still damp but at least it wasn't dripping as it had been when he'd got here.

'I'll see you out.' She led the way to the front door and when she turned to say goodbye discovered him standing right behind her. He slid both arms about her, pulling her even closer. 'Uh — what are you doing?'

'This,' he murmured, lowering his head to hers and capturing her lips. 'Something I've been longing to do since the first time I saw you.'

Jazz stood perfectly still, letting his mouth move over hers. It was a gentle kiss, not demanding in any way. She kissed him back, waiting for some sort of emotion, any sort of emotion. She hadn't been kissed in quite some time. Not by choice. She just hadn't met anyone who stirred her sufficiently to want to kiss him. But she felt no response now either. It was just a kiss — between friends, not potential lovers. Unexpectedly, another face floated in front of her mind's eye — Zak Rivers' face. She jerked away from Joel, exasperated beyond measure. That wretched man, always where he wasn't wanted.

'Sorry,' he said, manifestly not meaning it. 'Well, no, I'm not, actually. I enjoyed it — ' He studied her intently; knowingly. 'But clearly you didn't.'

'I'm tired, Joel. Sorry.' She gave a weak smile.

His expression cooled by several degrees in the face of her rebuff. 'I'll let you get to bed then.' He leant close to her again but this time made it just a brief peck on her forehead. It was a gesture of affection rather than desire. She felt a surge of guilt. He'd gone to the trouble of seeing her home and this was how she repaid him. She stood on her tiptoes and kissed his cheek. 'Again — thanks, Joel.'

He gave a wry smile. 'I'll see you soon.'

'Of course you will,' she too smiled, more warmly this time, 'we are neighbours, after all.'

Once he'd gone, she leant back against the door and closed her eyes. Joel was an attractive man. Why hadn't she been able to respond to him? Instead, the only face she'd been able to bring to mind had been that of Zak Rivers, and she didn't even like the man, for goodness sake. But, more importantly, she didn't trust him either. She must be more tired than she'd supposed. She'd get a good night's sleep and everything would look different in the morning.

7

But that wasn't the way things went.

She went to bed and, almost immediately, fell into a deep, dreamless sleep. At first, she didn't know what it was that had woken her. She blinked blearily at the clock on the bedside table. One thirty. She'd only been asleep for an hour or so. It was then that she heard it: music; more specifically, piano music. And it seemed to be coming from downstairs — from the dining room. That was where the piano was, after all.

She eased herself upright until she was half sitting, half lying — listening intently. Was this really happening, or was she still asleep and dreaming? The notes tinkled away, they sounded real enough. She pushed herself further upright. It couldn't be someone — here — in the house, could it — an intruder;

a burglar? But why would he be hanging around playing the piano — risking discovery? He'd grab what he wanted and leave again.

With a heart that was beginning to pound, she climbed out of bed and put on her dressing gown. She was in the process of tying the belt, when she realised the music had stopped. She stood still, ears strained to hear any sort of sound — anything at all — but the silence was absolute. Even the wind and rain had died away. Had she dreamt it, after all? She hadn't even been sure where it was coming from. Could it have simply been music drifting through the night? Carried on the wind from somewhere else? But apart from Joel's, there were no other houses nearby, and she couldn't imagine Joel playing music at this time of the night and certainly not loudly enough to be heard at Cliff House.

Still, at least it wasn't footsteps — Even so, she'd have to go and investigate; she'd never sleep if she didn't. Before she could lose her nerve, she walked out onto the landing and ran down the stairs. At the bottom, she stood and listened once more. Still no music, but she thought she heard something; a faint click. Where had it come from? She glanced around the hallway. The front door was still securely closed, the key sitting exactly where she'd left it on the table.

Gingerly, she made her way towards the dining room. The door stood open, as it always did. The room beyond was in darkness. She crept into the room, and flicked on the light switch. The room was instantly bathed in light. Her shoulders sagged with relief; there was no-one here. She wondered what she would have done if there had been someone?

She crossed to the piano. The lid was down over the keyboard and there was no indication of anyone having been there, playing it. She must have been dreaming, it was the only credible explanation. She swivelled, checking out the whole room. Nothing —

Still, seeing as she was down here now, she'd check the rest of the ground floor, just for peace of mind; she even looked inside the hall cupboard. There was a cricket bat propped up in one corner. She and Joel used to play with it, not that she'd been any good at hitting the ball. She pulled it out. It would make a very effective weapon if there should be an intruder hiding somewhere.

But her search uncovered nothing; everything was exactly as it should be. Which begged the question — if she hadn't been dreaming, and she still wasn't a hundred percent sure she had been — where had the music been coming from?

She went into the kitchen intending to check the on/off button on the small radio that she kept in there, in the faint hope that it hadn't been turned off completely and had somehow fleetingly switched itself back on. It seemed highly unlikely, but she pressed the button anyway. Music instantly filled

112

the room: piano music. Not the same piece that she'd heard earlier, but — coincidence or not?

She flicked the button off again. She was sure it had been properly off, so that wasn't the explanation. She went and leant against the Aga, arms crossed in front of her, surveying the room, a sensation of unease creeping through her. Yet everything looked as it should do. The cups that she and Joel had drunk from were still standing on the draining board — just as she'd left them. Her coat was still draped over a stool. There was no indication that anyone had been either in here or in the dining room. So, if she hadn't been dreaming, she must have imagined it. She ignored the nagging little voice within as it asked — but what about the footsteps? Did you imagine them too?

★   ★   ★

With the arrival of morning came pale blue skies and a wintry sunshine. She needed something to occupy herself with, she decided, something other than her own thoughts and anxieties; she'd ring the woman at the lifeboat shop — Mandy Richards — and see if she needed any help. As it was a gift shop, she presumed it would be open on a Sunday?

To think had always been to act as far as Jazz was concerned, so ten minutes and one phone call later she was on her way into St. Kernan. Mandy had breathed a heartfelt sigh of relief at Jazz's offer. 'Joan, who usually comes in today rang in sick. I'm on my own and I have to leave at lunchtime — '

So that's how Jazz found herself standing behind the counter in the small gift shop. Most of the other shops were open, she'd noticed, and the town was bustling, not only with local residents but also with people who looked like tourists. Clearly winter weekend breaks were popular.

As she had hoped she would be, she was kept busy and the day passed quickly and productively. Beth called in. 'I thought it was you I could see in here. How are you?'

And despite repeatedly telling herself that what had happened the night before had been nothing more than a dream, she found herself telling Beth about the piano music, and even the footsteps — Beth initially looked shocked, then deeply worried.

'It's being in that house on your own too much. I tell you what, come in for a cup of tea on your way home,' she invited. 'I'll buy us a nice cake each, the bakery's still open — it's more than time for a spot of self-indulgence, I'd say,' and with a wave and a beaming smile she was gone, murmuring under her breath, 'Well — I never did — not in all my life — piano music, indeed — and-and footsteps? The things we think we hear — '

And Jazz was more than ready for a cup of tea by the time she shut up shop. Mandy had told her to keep the key, she had a spare. Jazz wasted no time in getting to Beth's and she was very shortly knocking on the door of forty two. It was a very old house, older than Cliff House. Beth had told her that it was one of the original buildings in the ancient town, when it had been no more than a single street and a church.

'Come in, dear, the kettle's on,' was Beth's cheerful greeting. Jazz followed her inside, her gaze resting on the low beamed ceilings and small windows. There was even a door that Beth had told her led down to a cellar and a well.

'Now then,' Beth said, as she handed a cup of tea to Jazz, 'tell me again what happened last night.'

Jazz did so, trying to make light of it all, and portray the previous night's events as an extremely graphic dream, only to ruin her efforts by asking, 'You told me that Emily looked frightened when you found her. Do you have any idea at all why that would be so?'

'I wish I could say I did, my dear, but I don't. She never mentioned anything about piano music in the night — or

116

footsteps,' she took a cautious sip of her steaming tea, 'and I'm sure if there'd been anything of that nature going on, she would have. We'd been friends for so long, you see.'

'Did she still play the piano, do you know?'

'Sometimes, but she said her fingers weren't as supple as they used to be. Apart from that, though, I don't think she had the time — what with her business. Tell me, have you had any offers to buy that?'

'Yes, a fairly good one. I've accepted it. I can't run it.'

'That's a shame. It was very profit-able.'

Jazz shrugged. 'I know, but I'm not good on design like Emily was. She always had an eye for that sort of thing. You can tell from the way she's transformed Cliff House.'

'Ye-es, but still — '

A knock on the front door distracted Beth from whatever it was she'd been going to say. Jazz was relieved. She'd had an uncomfortable suspicion Beth had been about to urge her to hang on to the business. 'Now, who could that be, I wonder? I'm not expecting anyone — '

Jazz carried on drinking her tea and nibbling at the chocolate éclair which Beth had insisted she have.

'Oh — Mr Rivers,' she heard Beth exclaim. Jazz let the éclair drop back onto her plate. What on earth could Zak Rivers want with Beth?

'Oh, please, you were calling me Zak last night.'

'Oh well, all right. Zak. Come in, please. You're my second visitor so I've got a pot of tea all brewed.'

Beth bustled back into the kitchen, looking distinctly flustered. With her back to Zak, she raised her eyebrows at Jazz as if to say, 'Well, who would have thought it? Zak Rivers — ?' As for Zak, he was carrying the biggest bouquet of flowers that Jazz had ever seen. They would easily fill a couple, maybe three, vases. He handed them to Beth.

'Oh my,' Beth cried, her agitation instantly soothed at the unexpected generosity of the gift, 'how lovely. Look, Jazz, freesias — my favourites, and daffodils, jonquil, tulips — wherever did you get them? Not from St. Kernan, I'll be bound.'

Zak smiled at her, 'No, I had to venture a bit further afield. Thank heavens for Sunday opening — '

'They're gorgeous. Thank you very much,' and she hurriedly pulled a couple of vases from a cupboard, to fill them with water and carefully arrange the flowers.

'They're lovely,' Jazz murmured.

'If I'd known you'd be here, I'd have brought two lots of flowers,' he said.

'Why?' Jazz blurted. 'I've done nothing to deserve them.' She was having the most disturbing image — just as she'd had the night before — of him bending his head and kissing her. She metaphorically shook herself free of it. The very last man she wanted to kiss her was Zak Rivers. She was sure he was accustomed to kissing far more beautiful women than her. Women like Sara whom he'd been so obviously pleased to see the evening before.

'Just being here would be sufficient reason,' he said.

Was that sarcasm? Jazz eyed him, trying to determine from his expression what his emotion might be. Exasperatingly, and although he was looking straight at her, it revealed nothing.

'I assume you got home safely last night — with the ever faithful Scott nipping at your heels.'

This time, it was definitely sarcasm. Jazz didn't respond. She could be every bit as inscrutable as he was.

'Did he see you inside the house?

'He came in for a nightcap, actually — '

His eyes narrowed and his lips tightened.

' — and to dry off. We were both soaked — '

'Why? You both had cars, didn't you?'

'Yes, but the rain and wind were so

bad, we were drenched between leaving the cars and getting into the house.' Why was she explaining herself to him? And why did he seem to have that effect on her, of inducing her to say more than she wanted to? It was maddening.

'Of course, and where you're situated, you would get the worst of the weather,' he murmured.

'Exactly, so not the best location for a luxury hotel and its pampered guests — as I believe I pointed out to you once before.'

'So you did.' Again, he spoke so softly she had to strain to hear, 'and you'd probably be right.'

Hah, one up for her! Despite her jubilation, however, Jazz's senses sharpened at that. Was he implying that he'd given up trying to persuade her to sell Cliff House to him? But before she could ask, Beth was handing him a mug of tea with the words 'My Hero' printed in bright red across the front of it. Jazz saw Zak look at it and his mouth twitch with amusement, before

121

his eyes twinkled and he said, 'Thanks, Beth.' His glance moved immediately to Jazz, whereupon he slowly lowered his one eyelid in a wink, thus provoking a helpless gasp of mirth from her as they silently shared the joke. Beth remained completely oblivious to the comical side of it all, however, and said, 'Jazz has been getting some strange things happening — '

'Beth,' Jazz instantly protested, the last person she wanted to know about her problems was Zak Rivers, 'it's nothing — '

'Nonsense, not in your mind it isn't.' She looked back from Jazz to Zak.

'What things?'

The irrepressible Beth couldn't seem to stop herself, despite the glares in her direction from Jazz, 'footsteps crossing a bedroom, and — would you believe — piano music in the middle of the night.'

'What sort of piano music?'

'Um — ' Jazz was beginning to feel

extremely embarrassed about the whole thing, ' — something classical. I didn't recognise it.'

'How intriguing,' he murmured, 'a highbrow intruder.'

He was definitely being sarcastic now. Jazz couldn't mistake it. 'I must have been dreaming.' Now, he'd have her down as a silly, hysterical woman; one, moreover, who didn't know when she was dreaming and when she was awake. Why hadn't she simply laughed the whole thing off?

'Did you have a look round?' he demanded to know. All trace of amusement had vanished; it had given way to something that looked like genuine concern.

'Yes. There was no-one — nothing there — '

'So — you were sufficiently awake to get up and check everything; that seems to suggest you weren't dreaming. That you really did hear music.'

Jazz stared at him. That was the last thing she wanted to hear. Could he be deliberately feeding her fear; playing on it? For his own ends? Maybe she'd imagined the implication that he'd given up trying to get her to sell Cliff House? Or had he re-thought that in the light of what he'd just learnt? If that was so, then it meant he was a crafty and cruel opportunist, fully prepared to exploit any weakness of hers in order to get what he wanted: Cliff House.

'Well, I was awake then — clearly. But I must have dreamt the music and then woken up.'

He tilted his head to one side as he subjected her to a particularly intent stare. 'You don't seem the overly imaginative type.'

Huh! Jazz thought. What would he know?

'You know what I think?'

Jazz shook her head.

'I think it's being stuck out there — all on your own.' His expression sharpened. 'Was this after Scott left?

'Yes. I was in bed — as I said — '

'How long did Scott stay?'

'Long enough to have a hot drink and then — ' Her cheeks flamed at the memory of Joel's kiss.

Of course, Zak noticed. 'You're quite sure he left?'

'Wh-what do you mean? Of course I'm sure.' Was he implying that she was lying? That Joel had stayed the night?

'He could have hung around. Embarked upon a spot of extra-curricular activity?'

'He left. I saw him — What sort of extra-curricular activity?' There it was again, the insinuation that she and Joel had spent the night together.

'He could have somehow sneaked back in — played some music, you have a radio, don't you?'

She nodded. 'Oh, I see — But why — why would he do such a thing?'

'To try and scare you.'

'No, Joel wouldn't do that. Why would he?'

'Well, he and his boss have their eyes on Cliff House — ' he shrugged. 'If you up and left, they could buy it.'

'That theory would also apply to

you,' she blurted.

'Not my style — scaring women.'

'And neither is it Joel's,' she hotly said. 'In any case, how would he have got in, I'd locked the door.'

He said nothing for a moment. Then, 'You had turned the radio off properly, I suppose? It couldn't have somehow turned back on, could it?'

The change of subject was abrupt, startling Jazz, but also providing relief. She didn't want to dwell too long on the possibility of someone trying to scare her away. She said, 'I wondered that too, so I tried it. It had definitely been switched off, but — there was some piano music playing.'

'I wonder — coincidence or something more?' He sipped his tea, regarding her thoughtfully. 'Do you want me to come and give the place a once over? Check the attic, the cellar, that sort of thing — ?'

'There is no cellar.'

He looked surprised. 'Isn't there? I was under the impression there was. I thought I'd seen something somewhere — on a plan, a drawing — '

Where would Zak Rivers have seen a plan of Cliff House? Had he been doing some snooping? Knowing him as she was beginning to, she wouldn't be surprised. 'Emily would have shown me if there was.'

'One would have thought so, unless, of course, she didn't know about it. The entrance could have been sealed up, I suppose — Anyway, it might make you feel more secure if someone checks it all out.'

'I've checked everywhere myself. There's no evidence of a cellar, or of anyone having been inside the house who shouldn't have been. And I hardly think you'd find anything in the attic.'

Again, he shrugged. 'Okay. It was just a thought. But, Jazz, if you're ever frightened — and you are very isolated there, as I've pointed out more than once now.'

'Haven't you just?' she murmured. In

fact, he'd been at great pains to point it out.

He ignored that, if he'd even heard it that was, ' — just give me a call.'

'What? At one thirty in the morning?' She sounded incredulous, she knew, but she couldn't help it. The thought of Zak Rivers turning out at that time was simply too unbelievable to give serious consideration to.

'If you're frightened — or even just nervous — then yes, I could be with you in a matter of minutes.'

'That's very kind of you, Zak.' Beth broke in, in the absence of any indication of gratitude from Jazz.

But the truth was that all Jazz could think was — Zak Rivers was the last man she'd call, not least, because the thought of him — in her house — alone with her — in the middle of the night was an extraordinarily disturbing one.

8

'Changing the subject,' Zak then went on, 'what are you planning to do with yourself now that you're here?'

'I've not decided yet. I've promised to help out in the lifeboat shop, and on the carnival committee, but I could do with a real job. I've always been accustomed to working — I don't suppose you know of any vacancies anywhere.' She was reluctant to ask for any sort of favour from Zak Rivers but needs must — and a job would do more than anything else to distract her from thoughts of someone — anyone — trying to drive her from her home.

'I do, actually.'

'You do? What — here — in St. Kernan?'

'Just outside, at my place, in fact. My PA just left and I'm looking to replace her.'

Jazz stared at him. Was he offering her a job?

'What did you do in your last position?'

Unbelievably, he seemed to be doing just that. 'Well — um, everything, really — I worked for a firm of solicitors so — I typed legal documents, answered the phone, set up appointments — ' her voice tailed off. This was the last thing she'd expected — or wanted, come to that — Zak Rivers offering her a job. Mind you, working so closely with him would mean that she could keep an eye on precisely what he was up to; even, maybe, learn what his plans were with regards to her refusal to sell to him. The other side of the coin, however, was that it would provide him with yet more opportunity to pressure her into selling to him. She'd be more or less at his mercy if she wished to keep her job. 'When you say your place, what do you mean?'

'I mean my house. I run all my businesses from there. It's large enough that I can set aside rooms for offices and it's very convenient. No travelling to work and back.'

'I see. And what would I be expected to do?'

'Everything you did for your previous employer from the sound of it. Obviously legal documents wouldn't be involved. I'd want you to keep my diary, and there'd be quite a bit of computer work: correspondence — that sort of thing; fielding phone calls when I'm not around. The job's generally keeping me in order and organised. Accompany me if I need to go anywhere — to take notes of meetings, that sort of thing.'

'Well — I don't — '

Beth was looking at her expectantly. It was obvious what she thought Jazz should do: take the job.

Seeing her hesitating, Zak pulled a notepad from his jacket pocket and scribbled something on it. He then tore the sheet of paper off and handed it to her. 'Your salary,' he simply said.

Jazz looked at it, stunned by what

was written there. The amount dwarfed her previous salary.

'Well? Are you interested?'

Oh, for heaven's sake, go for it, she told herself. Where else would she find something this well paid, this diverse? She nodded. 'Okay.'

'Well, don't be too eager now, will you? Such enthusiasm might go to my head.'

'Sorry. It's just that I'm — well, surprised — ' and if she were truly honest, not at all sure that she was doing the right thing.

'I see.' His expression now was such that she wondered whether he too was having second thoughts. 'Well, maybe you could start tomorrow. The job's ten till four, five days a week, with an hour's lunch break. There will be the occasional spot of overtime, of course — '

'I don't start till ten?' What sort of a job was that, for heaven's sake? Part time, that's what. So why, in heaven's name, was he offering such a high salary?

'Yes. There's no need for an earlier start. I like to get a few things of my own done to begin with.'

She couldn't help wondering, what things? Bribing planning officers? Ringing girlfriends? Getting them out of the house — or, more likely, out of his bed — before she turned up? And what did he mean by the occasional spot of overtime? How occasional and for how long?

Before she could ask, however, he said, 'Okay. Tomorrow it is then.'

And that was it: all done and dusted. She'd got a job, an extremely well paid job at that, and if the salary meant a little bit of overtime now and again, well — she wasn't about to quibble.

Once he'd gone, Beth clasped her hands together against her chest. She was delighted. So much so, that one would think it was her who had the job. 'Well, what a surprise. I take it the salary was acceptable?'

'Oh yes, most acceptable. Almost treble my last one. Makes me wonder what — precisely — he wants me to do for it,' she muttered with a grim little smile.

'Oh, you don't need to worry about that. There's nothing dodgy about Zak Rivers — '

Now, how could Beth possibly know that? Mind you, she knew practically everything about almost everyone, so maybe Jazz shouldn't be too surprised that she knew that as well.

'Who was his previous PA? Do you happen to know?'

'No. She wasn't from St. Kernan, St. Austell, I think. I do find myself wondering why she left so suddenly though.' Beth wrinkled her brow.

So, she wasn't completely in the know then? Jazz mused. The trouble was Jazz was belatedly questioning that too. Maybe she should have asked him before blindly accepting the job?

She'd only been back at Cliff House for a little while when Joel turned up.

'Joel. What can I do for you?'

'Allow me to apologise.'

'Look — don't stand on the door-step, come in. Have a cup of tea, or a drink?'

'Um — I'll have a glass of wine if that's okay,' and he smiled somewhat sheepishly at her.

'I've got a bottle of Pinot Grigio in the fridge.'

'Perfect.' He followed her into the kitchen, a bit too closely for Jazz's comfort. She could feel the warmth of his breath upon the back of her neck, smell his aftershave. She'd always hated having her personal space invaded — other than by those most close to her.

'So — what do you want to apologise for?' She didn't know why she'd asked that. She knew very well what he wanted to apologise for. She deftly removed the cork from the bottle and filled a glass for him.

'For last night; I'm sorry for trying to rush you into something you clearly didn't want.'

'Oh, that.'

'Yes, that.' He gave a tight little smile. Obviously her casual manner had taken him aback.

'Don't think anymore about it, I haven't.'

'Well, that's put me well and truly in my place.'

'Sorry. I didn't intend it that way. You're a good friend, Joel, but that's as far as it goes — '

'Wow! Stick the knife in a bit further, why don't you?'

She had been a bit tactless, she conceded. Honest, but tactless. 'I'm sorry — '

'Yeah, well, I was sort of hoping that I'd become a bit more than just a friend.'

Jazz shrugged. She didn't want to hurt him anymore than she clearly already had. 'It's early days yet. Who can say how things will turn out?'

He looked fractionally cheered by that. 'Do you mean I can hope?'

'I don't know. We've only just met again after — fifteen, sixteen years? I don't know you. You were a mere boy, I was even younger. These things take time — for me, at any rate.'

'Is there someone else?'

'No.'

'No-one you've left behind; pining, lovelorn?'

'What is this? Some sort of inquisition?' she quipped. 'I wasn't in any sort of relationship — and haven't been for a while.'

'So — you're a fussy kind of gal, then?'

She wasn't sure whether he was joking or criticising. There was a strange expression on his face: unidentifiable. It made her realise how little she really knew about Joel.

'You could say that, I suppose.' She frowned; things were beginning to feel strained; edgy. 'I don't go out with just anyone — '

'Well, I'd hardly describe myself as just anyone.' He sounded positively offended now.

Jazz decided a change of subject was

overdue, before she upset him beyond repair. 'I have some news,' she told him. 'I've got a job. I start tomorrow.'

'That was quick — where?'

'At Zak Rivers' place; he needs a new PA.'

'Zak Rivers? Are you mad?'

'I don't think so — no.'

'It'll just give him even more opportunity to pressure you into selling to him — ' He was watching her intently now, his eyes narrowed with speculation. 'You do know why his last PA left, don't you?'

She shook her head.

'Sexual harassment.'

'Sexual harassment?'

'Yeah.'

Jazz felt her heart give a sickening jolt. Why hadn't Beth known this? God, she knew practically everything else about Zak Rivers. 'Wh-who told you that?'

'No-one actually told me. It's all round the town.'

'So, there's no real evidence then?

138

It's just gossip?'

'Well, gossip can be pretty reliable — '

'Oh, Joel, gossip is never reliable.' She didn't know whether to be relieved by the fact that the source of the rumour was no more than hearsay, or whether to be seriously worried that there might actually be some substance behind it. Maybe she should ring Zak and tell him she'd changed her mind?

'Well, just be careful — promise?'

'Okay, I promise.'

Once Joel had gone again, she sat, finishing her own glass of wine and considering what he'd told her. It did make her wonder about the nature of the occasional overtime Zak had referred to? She frowned down into her glass, as if somehow she would discover the answer to her question within its depths. Yet, for all his faults — and let's face it, he had a few — Jazz couldn't envisage Zak Rivers as some sort of sexual predator. Scaremonger — yes, she'd already had a taste of that, but sexual predator — no.

Oh well, she sighed, she'd accepted his job offer now so she'd give it a chance. But, at the first sign of anything even remotely questionable, she'd be out of his house so fast, a greyhound at full pelt wouldn't be any competition at all.

By the next morning, Jazz was still uncertain whether she was doing the right thing. Nonetheless, she'd decided to give the job — and Zak Rivers — a fair trial. Keep it professional, she told herself. With that in mind, she dressed in the sort of clothes she'd worn for her previous job: a navy blue suit and crisp white blouse. He'd quickly get the message, she was sure — that she was there simply to work. Zak Rivers wasn't stupid. He wouldn't have got where he was today if he had been. That thought provided a grain of comfort for her as she climbed into her car, but that's all it was — a grain.

Determined to begin as she meant to go on, she was ringing the doorbell to the Old Manor House on the dot of ten. But if she was prompt, Zak sadly wasn't. She had to ring twice more before the door was finally jerked open by a plump woman, a woman who looked distinctly ruffled; harassed, even. Her skirt was creased and her blouse gaping where a button had come undone.

Jazz's heart sank. Oh no. While she'd been standing on the doorstep, Zak had been — She stared at the woman. She didn't look like Zak's type at all; the total opposite, in fact, to the svelte and glamorous Sara who'd been at Beth's party on Saturday night. She also looked several years older than him.

'Sorry, sorry — ' the woman blurted, tucking a wayward strand of hair behind her ear with one hand, while with the other, she busily smoothed down her decidedly creased skirt. 'You must be Jazz. Mr Rivers did say you'd be coming.'

Jazz gave a nervous smile. What sort of household she was about to enter?

'You must be wondering why I didn't answer straight away — ' Two dogs appeared behind her, bounding into the hallway, ears perked, tails waving: two beautiful Red Setters, 'and here's the reason — ' she grinned down at the bouncing animals, fondly patting the head of the one to reach her first.

Jazz knew a moment's unutterable relief. She'd been on the verge of climbing back into her car and leaving as promptly as she'd arrived.

'The rascals wouldn't let me out of the kitchen — '

'Petrus, Napoleon,' a stern voice came from behind the woman. It was Zak. 'Get back here — heel — heel, I say, you silly animals.'

Petrus, Napoleon? She hadn't had Zak down as a pretentious man: arrogant, yes; totally self-confident, another yes; ruthless, even — but pretentious? No.

But whatever his reason for choosing such names, at his authoritative tones, the dogs did precisely as he commanded. They ran back to their owner and settled at his heels. 'My sister's dogs,' he said. 'I'm caring for them for a month or so while she's off gallivanting. Ridiculous names, aren't they? Thank heavens, she's back later today and they can return to her.'

Jazz deduced from that that he'd all too accurately read her expression of disdain. She didn't respond to his question, however. It wouldn't do to criticise her employer's sister within the first few moments of the job — even if he had.

'They're still young,' he went on, 'and virtually untrained, and poor Thelma here has been on the receiving end of their bad behaviour. Sorry, Thelma — ' and he smiled apologetically.

'That's okay, I'm getting used to them now.'

Zak opened a door on the far side of the hallway and ordered the dogs through it. He then closed the door behind them.

Zak turned back to Jazz. 'Now, let me

143

introduce you properly to Thelma, my housekeeper. Thelma, this is Jazz.'

'Yes, I realised that.' Thelma smiled at Jazz, her easy friendliness only too evident. 'Now that order's been restored, would you like a cup of coffee — to start the day?'

'Thank you, Thelma,' Zak said before Jazz could respond, 'bring a pot and two cups to my study, would you? Jazz, please come this way.'

He led her into a room that couldn't be mistaken for anything other than what it was: a man's study. The furniture was upholstered in leather the exact shade of a walnut and what looked like genuinely old oak panelling covered the walls; there was nothing of the fake 'distressed' look about any of it. Jazz wasn't in the least bit surprised. She couldn't imagine Zak Rivers wanting anything less than the authentic, real thing around him.

She took her time looking around, taking in the huge desk, the — as she'd

already decided — original oak panelled walls, the oatmeal-coloured carpet
and leather armchairs. Bookcases lined
an entire wall, and three ceiling-high
French windows filled another. Through
these, she could see extensive gardens;
the large beds, naturally, were mostly
empty of plants at this time of the year,
but she had no trouble visualising the
beauty that must surround the house
come summertime.

Zak indicated that she should sit in
one of the armchairs; he took the other.
'Well, as you can see, this is my office
where you'll invariably find me when
I'm at home. Despite my base being
here, I do have to conduct a great deal
of business outside of the house.' He
was business-like and abrupt. Evidently,
she wasn't the only one who was
starting as she meant to go on. So was
Zak. It came as a considerable relief.
Such formality suited her down to the
ground. If things remained like that,
then she'd be more than content. 'As
soon as we've had coffee, I'll show you

your office next door and detail what I want you to do today — '

As if his words had summoned her, the door opened and Thelma came in, bearing a large tray upon which sat a cafetiere of coffee and two bowl-like cups, as well as sugar and cream. She set it down on the low table that lay midway between Zak and Jazz and poured out the steaming black liquid before exiting the room once more. The delicious aroma filled the room. Jazz breathed it in. She loved the smell of freshly made coffee. In fact, she sometimes found the aroma preferable to the taste of the actual coffee.

'Help yourself to whatever you want,' Zak commanded.

'I like it black — thank you.'

'Okay. So — let's get down to work. If you'd get your pad out — '

She gnawed at her bottom lip. She should have thought of bringing a pad with her. Now she looked inept and amateurish. Not a good start. 'I haven't brought one with me. Sorry.'

'No problem.' He stood up and walked to his desk, whereupon he slid open a drawer and pulled one out. 'I always keep a few handy.' He strode back to her and handed it over, along with a pen.

'Okay — now I thought you could start with — ' and he proceeded to outline a list of tasks that would keep her fully occupied for the best part of a week, never mind today. 'And then, this afternoon — '

She stared up at him — this afternoon? Did he expect her to finish the first lot of tasks in a morning? Who did he think she was, for heaven's sake — Superwoman?

'Aren't you going to take any notes? There's rather a lot to remember.'

'Yes — of course.' What the hell had she taken on? Her confidence in her ability to do the job plummeted.

'On second thoughts, tomorrow will do — '

No wonder he was willing to pay such a high salary. She was obviously expected to earn every last darned penny of it. Some of this — she looked down at her pad, quite unable to hide her dismay — would take days to do and he was expecting it by tomorrow.

A small sound had her glancing up at him again. His mouth was twitching, his eyes gleaming. He knew damn well she wouldn't be able to complete the work he'd set her by tomorrow. So — was all this yet another tactic to undermine her; undermine her confidence in herself; to drive her away, in fact? Was that why he'd offered her this job? Anger began to seep into her. For two pins, she'd throw the notepad at him.

'I'm kidding. No-one — short of a miracle worker, that is, and I assume you're not one of those — could do that lot in under a week.'

She smiled weakly at him, somehow resisting the even stronger urge now to throw something at him; something a darn sight heavier than a mere notepad.

9

'I like to plan the work a few days in advance,' he said. That irritating gleam had gone from his eye; in fact, it was as if it had never been there, 'then, if I'm not around, you know what needs to be done and not have to wait for me to turn up. There's just one more thing. I shall want you to accompany me to Exeter this afternoon.' He spoke with as much calm as if he'd just announced he was going to have another cup of coffee. Jazz felt her mouth drop open — Exeter? 'I have an appointment and I'll need you to take notes of everything that is said, word for word. I don't want anyone trying to argue about the decision that is taken, what was said and why at a later date. How's your shorthand?'

'Um — ' a bit rusty she was tempted to say, it had been some time since she'd used it. Her last job hadn't called for it very often, ' — okay.' She'd never been that brilliant at it, truth to tell, but, somehow, had always managed to get by. She could write most of it down — even if it was in her own rather peculiar form of symbols; it was reading it back later that sometimes stumped her. Maybe she should tell him that?

However, before she could do so, he was speaking again. 'Good. Be ready to leave by one thirty, please.' And the moment for confession was gone — especially as he had reverted to the efficient, business-like, slightly intimidating employer that he'd been at the start. She'd just have to trust in her ability to get by, that and a generous dollop of luck. He started to get to his feet, and then stopped.

'I know it's your first day but obviously I'll need you to work a bit later than four o'clock. I'll treat you to dinner on the way back — as recompense,' he concluded with a smile.

Jazz stared at him, astonished at his offer, and more than a little appalled at the very notion of sitting down to a meal with Zak Rivers. What on earth would they talk about, just the two of them? However, it seemed unavoidable. The drive to Exeter alone would take a couple of hours — each way — and that's only if there were no traffic holdups anywhere. What time was he planning to get back by, for goodness sake — midnight? If so, that was considerably more than a 'bit later than four o'clock'.

'B-but Exeter's a good two hours drive — ' she couldn't resist saying, even though she was well aware that he would know that.

'Is that a problem?' The smile had been extinguished by a look that had all the properties of a glacier. The wretched man was turning into a chameleon, warm and friendly one minute, cold as ice the next; all, she suspected, designed to keep her off balance and uncertain. Why on earth

151

had she agreed to work for him? She must have been mad. Maybe she should just hand in her notice right now? 'Just so that there's no misunderstanding, Jazz, I do demand one hundred percent of effort from my employees. It's why I offer such a high wage.' He considered her for a moment. 'I did tell you that there'd be the odd spot of overtime.'

Yes, but she hadn't anticipated it happening on her very first day. And, let's face it, four-five hours was hardly a spot of overtime. It was practically a full day's work. However, he was perfectly correct, he had been up front about it, so she supposed she had no real grounds for complaint. 'Of course it's not a problem.' Her tone now was every bit as frigid as his. Not for anything would she allow him to detect her uncertainty, her lack of confidence; her sheer horror at the prospect of all that time — alone — with him.

'After all, there's no-one waiting at home for you, is there?'

Something occurred to her then.

Maybe this — demanding unpredict-ability had been the real reason for his previous PA's departure? Not sexual harassment as the gossips had it. That seemed much more plausible. Because on current evidence, it looked as if Zak Rivers was going to prove a hard taskmaster. Was she up to it? Appar-ently, she'd have to be — if she wanted to retain her job. He'd made that more than evident. Jazz shook her head.

'Okay, I've got to go out now, so I'll show you your office and where everything is and then leave you to it.'

Jazz swallowed. Crunch time had arrived. She just hoped she was up to the demands that she guessed were about to be made upon her.

★　★　★

Jazz sat at her desk, staring at the computer screen. She'd been working non-stop for a good two hours and she hadn't made more than a dent in the inordinate amount of work that Zak had given her. Of course, she would be slow to start with, just until she got used to things, but even so, there was still a huge amount to get through.

At twelve thirty exactly, she began the sandwich that she'd brought with her. At twelve thirty five, the office door opened and Thelma walked in, carrying a tray upon which Jazz saw a bowl of steaming soup, a bread roll and a dish of what looked like chicken salad.

'Oh no, Ms Wheatley, that will never do.' Thelma regarded her meagre sandwich with scorn. 'We always provide lunch for our staff. Zak is most particular about that. No-one can work with an undernourished body, he says.'

So, Thelma called her employer by his Christian name. 'That does smell absolutely delicious, Thelma. And — please — call me Jazz.'

'Thank you, I will. Now, you be a good girl and eat it all,' the kindly woman said, before disappearing once more.

Jazz chuckled to herself. Thelma

obviously fancied herself as the proverbial mother hen; still — it felt nice to be
someone's chick. It was a feeling not
often experienced by Jazz, at least not
since the last time she'd stayed with
Emily. Serena, her mother, had never
been the motherly sort. Both Jazz and
Flick had needed to be independent
and self-sufficient from a fairly young
age. Not that it had done either of them
any harm; rather the reverse, in fact.
They'd grown into responsible young
women — well, Jazz had, hopefully. She
wasn't so sure about Flick. Flick could,
at times, be extremely irresponsible
— as in the case of spending, in
advance, an inheritance she hadn't been
destined to receive, and all within a
week or so. That had been no mean
achievement.

At one fifteen, Zak strode back into
her office, bulging briefcase in one
hand, keys jangling in the other. In
contrast to earlier that morning, when
he'd been wearing a sweater and jeans,
he was now smartly attired in a dark

grey suit, white shirt and maroon and grey striped tie. He had a camel overcoat slung carelessly about his shoulders.

'Ready?' he demanded to know.

'Almost — ' He was earlier than he'd said.

'Well, finish up while I'm bringing the car round to the front door. I want to get on. We've got a considerable journey ahead of us and the weather doesn't sound good.'

Jazz wondered what he meant. She hadn't seen a forecast in days. Sadly, she didn't have to wonder for long. Before they'd been travelling for an hour, the first flakes of snow were falling.

'I didn't think it snowed down here,' she remarked. 'Let's hope it's not much and quickly melts again.'

Without looking at her, Zak said — quite casually, 'We're to expect two to three inches apparently, which will freeze later.'

'What?' She turned her head and

stared at him in dismay. 'B-but why did we set off?'

Whether one was driving a Range Rover or not — which they were — negotiating frozen, snowy roads could prove far from easy. In fact, it could turn out to be positively tricky. Not surprisingly, she found herself hoping that Zak was a skilful driver, or who knew what sort of trouble they might find themselves in? She didn't fancy being stuck in snow — maybe for hours — in the confines of a vehicle, with just him for company. It would make sitting across a dinner table a breeze by comparison.

'Because I said I'd be there and it's a crucial meeting. A lot hangs on it — I'm negotiating for a prime site upon which to build an entire holiday complex. There's intense competition for it and I intend to be the one who gets it. We can always stay overnight. I've already booked two rooms in a hotel in case we need them.'

Jazz stared, dumbstruck. 'B-but I've

got no overnight things with me — '

'Well, you can buy them.' He spoke impatiently, as if her concerns were simply too trivial to worry about. 'I'm sure a 5-star hotel, which it is, will have everything you need,' and he calmly carried on driving as if he hadn't just dropped the proverbial bombshell upon her.

By the time they reached the outskirts of Exeter, the snow was getting deeper by the minute. In fact, at one point they were driving through what amounted to blizzard conditions. Thankfully, Zak proved himself a skilful driver, handling the Range Rover as if he'd spent his entire life driving through snow storms.

It took them only minutes to locate the building they sought, whereupon Zak climbed from the car and walked round to Jazz's door and opened it. Jazz regarded the three — or maybe four inches of snow with abject horror. Thank goodness she'd had the forethought to put a warm coat over her suit that morning, but her shoes were going to be totally inadequate for such conditions, and they were her best ones. Expensive suede with slim heels, they were going to be totally ruined. A surge of anger engulfed her then. The sheer arrogance and — and complete disregard for someone else's comfort and trouble was mind blowing.

But as if reading her thoughts, he opened the rear car door and pulled out a pair of very expensive-looking, fleece-lined boots. He thrust them at her. 'Put these on. They may be slightly large but they'll make walking a whole lot easier and much more comfortable.'

Speechlessly, Jazz took them and slipped off her shoes to slide her feet into them. Miraculously, they were her size; they also looked brand new. Had he bought them for her, knowing the sort of weather they could be facing? If he had, it certainly undermined her preconceptions about him. She wriggled her toes inside them. The leather was so supple, she didn't feel as if she had boots on; they were like the softest slippers, with the same degree of warmth and comfort. She slanted a glance at him. He was constantly surprising her. Only someone who was kind and thoughtful would have done this.

Whatever his reasons, suddenly he was holding out a hand to her. She grasped it and gingerly climbed down from her seat. Throughout their walk into the building, Zak kept a tight hold of her, a couple of times practically lifting her as the icy ground proved almost impossible to walk over, despite the boots on her feet. She squinted through the fast falling snow. They'd never make it back this evening.

*　*　*

Two hours later they were leaving the building once more. Zak had revealed what an astute business man he was, securing the site he wanted, at the price he wanted, against — at one point it had seemed to Jazz — insuperable odds. He was indeed ruthless as Joel had mentioned, with a mind that could cut as smoothly and sharply as a well honed hatchet. He'd literally sliced through any opposition with logic and well reasoned argument.

'Well, that went exactly as I'd hoped,' he commented as they battled through the still falling snow to reach the car. Jazz could barely catch her breath, let alone speak. The wind whipped about her, swirling the flakes until she seemed to be swallowing them each time she opened her mouth to speak. In the end, she gave up and remained silent. 'Did you get it all down?' he unexpectedly asked.

Jazz took a deep breath and managed to part her lips sufficiently to mumble, 'yes.' As it was several snowflakes blew into her mouth, melting immediately on her tongue. All she needed in the aftermath of that confident 'yes' was the ability to read her notes back. She sent up a silent prayer that she'd have more luck doing that than she had the last time she'd used shorthand. Then, she made a complete fool of herself.

'Good. You can read it back to me when we get to the hotel, because there's no way we'll make it back to St. Kernan in this. You can put it all on computer then tomorrow when we get back to the office.'

Oh no! She'd hoped for some time alone to make more detailed notes of what had been actually said at the meeting while it was still fresh in her mind. From what Zak had just said, she clearly wasn't going to be allowed it. Her stomach lurched at the mere notion of the ordeal that lay ahead of her.

So wrapped up in her anxiety was she, that she barely registered Zak's effortless and skilful negotiation of the treacherous roads. It would be pointless protesting that she'd rather go home; the weather had rendered that impossible. There was at least six inches of snow by this time. She simply hoped that the hotel would be able to provide a change of underwear at least. The hotel bathroom would provide the necessary toiletries, especially a 5-star hotel. As for makeup, she always carried the bare essentials in her handbag — just in case. And this was most certainly a 'just in case' situation.

Sure enough, the first thing she spotted upon walking into the hotel reception area was a shop selling just what she needed.

'Buy what's necessary,' Zak said, 'and get them to charge it to my bill. I'll get us a drink in the bar — something I'm desperately in need of.'

Jazz almost ran into the shop, her head spinning at what lay ahead of her. Supposing she couldn't read her notes — what then? She dragged out the purchase of the undergarments she needed for as long as she could, but, in the end, knew she could postpone the moment of reckoning no longer. Knowing Zak as she was starting to, she wouldn't put it past him to come to the shop to find her.

Slowly, apprehensively, she made her way to the bar and there was Zak, sitting at a table in the far corner of the room. He was leafing through a copy of The Financial Times, and didn't look up until she was practically on top of him. He eyed the small bag she was carrying. 'Got all you need then?'

'Yes.'

'Good. Now, what would you like to drink?' He waved a hand and a waiter instantly materialised at the table. She'd always envied people the ability to do that. Only a very few had it, and she most certainly wasn't one of them. And it wasn't only the waiter that had leapt to do his bidding, a couple of women in the bar looked as if they'd be only too happy to do the same.

'White wine, please — dry.' Maybe a drink would improve her shorthand skills? It was certainly worth a try. On the other hand, of course, it could well obliterate them.

'Certainly, Madam,' the waiter said,

and went off to fetch the drink.

'Got your notes?' Zak asked.

Good grief! Couldn't he let her have a mouthful — or five — of her wine first? She opened her handbag and pulled out her pad. She opened it to the page where her notes began. There were a couple of dozen pages in all. She stared at the first page, before hurriedly turning to the second: none of it made sense. She frowned and went back to the beginning again.

'Is there a problem?'

'Of course not,' she blurted. 'I was simply getting my breath back.'

Zak relaxed back into his seat, glass in hand, a frown tugging at his brow as he waited for her to begin. Had he guessed she couldn't read it?

She swallowed. 'Okay,' mutely adding, please God — let me be able to do this.

And then, suddenly, haltingly, she was reading her notes. Her confidence surged and she continued with increasing speed and accuracy. She finished and snapped her pad shut with a triumphant smile.

'That's a relief.' His tone was an ironical one. 'You had me worried there for a while.'

Jazz lifted her head in the air and airily said, 'I can't imagine why.'

10

She and Zak had arranged to meet again in the bar before dinner. This time Zak had a large glass of white wine waiting for her. She couldn't help wondering — was this an attempt to get her drunk? The question revived her earlier fears of sexual harassment.

However, when he glanced up at her, there was no indication of anything out of the ordinary within his eyes. 'Is your room okay? Got everything you need?'

She nodded, sitting down and lifting the glass to her lips. In the same second her stomach emitted an extremely noisy growl.

'Oh dear,' he murmured, 'I think we'd better see about feeding you — before you fade away. Let's go through to the restaurant,' and he picked up the glass which she'd replaced upon the table before waving her ahead of him.

The food, as she'd expected it would be, was delicious and Jazz enthusiastically cleared her plate, before glancing up, to encounter Zak's slightly bemused gaze.

'I do like a woman who eats well,' was all he said however.

Jazz felt the colour creep up her face. Was he implying she was a pig? 'Sorry — '

'Don't be. Would you care for seconds?' and, without waiting for her answer, he waved the waiter over.

'Oh no — really — ' Jazz's face burned even more hotly. He did think she was greedy — But she'd been so hungry — ravenous, in fact.

But it was with a small, sideways smile at her, that he said to the waiter, 'Dessert menu, please.'

He'd been teasing her. This — this humorous side of him was the last thing she'd expected. It unnerved her slightly. Especially when he sat, silently watching her debate the merits of a gorgeous sounding Crème Brulee and a home-made chocolate mousse — she adored both — before saying abruptly, 'We'll have one of each.'

Gradually, as they talked and ate, Jazz relaxed, whether as a result of his unexpected geniality or — due solely to her nervousness in his company — the greater than normal amount of wine she'd consumed, she couldn't have said. They even discovered that they had a few things in common: a love of reading, classical music as well as some of the modern stuff — good food, as had been amply demonstrated that evening. Zak even went so far as to admit that he enjoyed cooking — when Thelma allowed him to that was. He did glance at her at one point and say, 'No more night-time music, I hope.'

'Oh — that. I've put it down to a particularly vivid dream — '

She had no wish to discuss what was happening. She wanted to forget it all for a few hours. It would also spoil what was turning out to be an extremely enjoyable evening — much to her amazement.

Finally, she leant back in her seat with a groan. 'Oh dear, I'm so full. I don't think I'll be able to move from this table.'

Zak's eyes gleamed at her. 'Well, I can see I may have to carry you, in that case.'

'Do you think you're strong enough?' She tilted her head back and laughed at him, pearly teeth showing between her parted lips, and then watched — in fascination — as his eyes darkened, and his mouth also parted slightly, his hooded gaze roaming over her flushed cheeks and shining eyes, and down onto her arched throat — It was as if he were physically touching her. Her body tingled, her senses were thrown into turmoil.

'Come on,' he suddenly, almost brusquely, said, at the same time getting to his feet, 'let's get you to bed — '

Jazz heard herself giggle. Dear God.

Whatever had got into her? Such girly behaviour was most unlike her. But then, as if to compound her foolishness, as she tried to stand she found herself losing her balance. Zak's arm immediately shot out, grabbing hold of her, before snaking around her waist, to help her out of the restaurant.

'I ca-an m-manage, thank you — ' she breathlessly stammered.

'That's not how it looks from where I'm standing.'

She stared up at him; her head was spinning. She stumbled. She was losing it. It could be the only explanation for what she said next. 'Well, I-I think it might be best if — ' She gave a soft hiccup.

Zak chuckled. 'If — what?'

'Well, I-I make it a pol-policy to never, ever — not under any circumstances — to con-con-sort with my boss.'

'I think that's a very wise decision.'

She slanted a glance up at him. His eyes had darkened again and were all but closed. 'How can you see with eyes that are closed?' she blurted with the sort of candour that only came with intoxication.

'I can see all I need to.' He ushered her into the lift and leaned her against the wall as he pressed the button for their floor. Then he swung back to her. His eyes were still half closed as he watched her.

Jazz was engulfed then by the most acute yearning for him to kiss her. She leant towards him, raising her face to his, and then watched his face pale as he caught her by the tops of her arms, drawing her close for an infinitesimal second and bending his head to fleetingly capture her lips, before he seemed to recover himself and roughly thrust her away from him. At that precise second, the lift bell sounded, heralding their floor. 'Saved by the bell,' she thought she heard him mutter beneath his breath.

She groaned in disappointment.

'Jazz,' Zak softly said, 'I don't make a

habit of kissing intoxicated women, I like them to be fully aware of what they're doing. Come on,' and he ushered her, none too gently, from the lift and walked her briskly to her bedroom door. 'Give me your key.' He unlocked her door and almost pushed her inside. 'In you go — ' the words were harshly spoken. 'I'll see you in the morning, eight o'clock for breakfast.' And with that, he was gone, leaving Jazz standing, dazed at the speed with which he'd taken his leave of her.

★ ★ ★

Morning arrived all too soon for Jazz and with it the mother of all headaches. She struggled into a sitting position and looked down over herself, at her crumpled suit and blouse; she must have tumbled onto the bed and instantly fallen asleep. There was only one thing for it. She undressed and made a mad dash for the bathroom, where she turned on the shower, hard and cold. She stood beneath it for a full ten minutes, until she was shivering and more or less back to normal, and it was only then, that the memories of the previous evening began to manifest themselves. Memories of wanting to kiss Zak, actually leaning towards him; he couldn't have mistaken her invitation — an invitation he had turned down, apart from that fleeting kiss.

She covered her eyes with hands that shook. Whatever must he think? He'd had to push her away — How on earth was she going to face him after that? She dared a peep through the window, and saw that at least one thing had gone her way. The snow had all but melted overnight; all that remained was grey slush.

What time was it? She dimly recalled Zak mentioning something about breakfast at eight o'clock. It was just after seven thirty. Swiftly, she redressed in her crumpled suit and blouse, smoothing it as best she could with her hands. In the absence of a hairbrush

— that was the one thing the hotel didn't supply — she ran her fingers through her hair, tugging the knotted strands apart and forcing them into some sort of shape. She finished with a generous layer of makeup, hoping it would camouflage any suggestion of a hangover.

With a head that still ached, she finally made it to the dining room at three minutes past eight. Zak saw her coming and got to his feet. His expression gave nothing away at all as he quietly said, 'Good morning.'

Jazz didn't know whether to be relieved by that or not. He could be saving his condemnation of her actions until later — when they were in the car and alone?

'I've ordered coffee. I hope that's okay.' The words 'you look as if you need it' were left unsaid.

'Thank you, that's fine.' She hesitated, but then couldn't stop herself; the words literally cascaded from her. 'I want to apologise — '

'Apologise — what for?'

'For last night — '

'You have nothing to apologise for, Jazz. You drank a little too much wine; my fault entirely for irresponsibly topping up your glass.'

He was being the perfect gentleman, gallantly taking the blame for what had happened.

'Now — sit down,' he urged her. 'Have a look at the menu. Some food will make all the difference, I'm sure.'

And it did. Once again, she swiftly cleared her plate, even going so far as to mop up the last smear of egg yolk with a corner of toast.

'You'll be pleased to know the snow's gone, so we can set off for home as soon as you're finished,' he eventually said.

'Yes, I know. I looked out first thing. I couldn't believe it. I was afraid we might be stuck here — '

The subsequent tightening of his mouth made Jazz all too conscious of the tactlessness of her remark. She'd made it sound as if the last thing in the world that she wanted was to be forced to spend any more time than necessary with him.

'Um — I di-didn't mean — ' she lamely began. Good grief — and after he'd been so nice about last night. 'S-sorry.'

But he ignored her pathetic attempt at an apology, and instead got to his feet. 'So — if you're ready, shall we go?'

* * *

Upon their arrival in St. Kernan, Jazz said, 'Could you drop me at Cliff House first? I really do need to change my clothes.'

'Yes, of course.' He spoke absently, all the time staring straight ahead. They'd barely exchanged a word, never mind a look, during the long drive back. It was as if their rapport of the evening before had never existed. She'd really blotted her copybook — mind you, as she'd decided once before, Zak had all the properties of a chameleon, changing mood at the drop of a hat. How on earth was she going to work for someone like that? Of course, she might not have to — after her behaviour of the night before. He might sack her. That could possibly make it the shortest term of employment in history.

'I'll wait for you,' he said, which did seem to indicate that maybe she still had a job?

'There's no need — '

He turned his head to look at her; his expression was an unfathomable one. 'Are you going to walk to the manor house then? Because your car's still there — or had you forgotten?'

'Of course it is.' Now, he'd think she was stupid as well as cheap. 'Okay — I won't be long. Ten minutes at most — '

He shrugged. 'Take as long as you wish, I've got some reading to do. I can do it here just as easily as back at the house.'

'Um — do you want to come inside?'
'No.'

His immediate response suggested to Jazz that he wasn't about to risk her trying to kiss him again. She did the only thing she could; she turned and sped into Cliff House. Once upstairs, she tore off her suit and blouse, now creased almost beyond redemption, and pulled out a pair of warm wool trousers and a cashmere sweater. She then slipped a warm gilet over it all. Next, she grabbed a coat from the hall cupboard and slipped her feet into a pair of her own boots. She packed a pair of shoes in her handbag for wear inside the manor house, and as she'd promised, was walking back to Zak's car within ten minutes.

'Well,' Zak said as she took her seat alongside him once more, 'a woman who means what she says. Astonishing — '

11

To her surprise, Zak didn't dismiss her and her second day at work proved considerably less eventful than her first had been. Zak took her to his house and then went on to an appointment somewhere else. After just a day, she hadn't got to grips with his diary, so she had no idea where he'd gone. In fact, she hadn't even glimpsed the diary in question, leading her to presume that he must keep it in his own office.

Thelma greeted her warmly. 'Come into the kitchen and have a cup of coffee.'

Jazz followed Thelma into a massive, high-ceilinged room, all done out with apricot and ivory walls, rust-coloured worktops, and enough stainless steel appliances to furnish the kitchen of an average size restaurant. If the rest of the house had been renovated in keeping with its period, this room was the exact opposite. Every mod con known to man — and woman — was to be seen here. The whole of one wall was made up of stainless steel ovens — she counted four in all — and, as if they weren't enough, in a recess in another wall sat a massive Aga. A central island contained a sink with space age taps, an eight ring hob and a built-in deep fat fryer. Four high stools sat along the one side which obviously served as a breakfast bar.

'Wow!' Jazz breathed.

Thelma pulled out one of the high stools and said, 'Sit down. I'll show you the rest of the house if you like after we've had our coffee.'

'Oh, yes please.'

'Zak's done wonders with it. It was fairly decrepit when he bought it.'

'Have you worked for him for long?'

'Oh, now — let me see — nine-ten years; he was just twenty five then and already a relatively rich man. I moved here with him from his last place.'

'Where was that?'

'Hampshire: a village called Lower Compton.'

'I've never heard of it. So — how long's he been here?'

'Just over four years. He told me that when he was a boy he used to come down here with his parents on holiday; he loved it then — '

'Where are his parents?'

'They're still in Hampshire. His father's just retired and has handed his business over to Zak.'

'So — ' Jazz sipped her coffee, 'is Zak a good employer?'

'Oh yes. You need have no worries on that score. Why — when my mother was so ill, he did everything he could to help, even down to paying for private nursing care for her. He's a lovely man — '

Jazz stared down into her cup. She was hearing about a very different side of Zak to the one that Joel had painted. And she'd seen, at first hand, how thoughtful he could be — evidence, the boots he'd bought for her.

'Why did his last PA leave?'

'She had some family problems.'

'So — it wasn't some sort of row then?'

'Good gracious, no. That's not Zak's style at all. I've never met a more understanding man. Now — if you've finished your coffee, I'll give you the grand tour.'

'Are you sure Zak won't mind?' What if he returned and discovered her poking around? That would be almost as embarrassing as her behaviour of the evening before.

'Oh no, he's very proud of it all.'

And within a few minutes, Jazz could see why. The drawing room was to die for. Done out in ivory, lemon and duck egg blue, it was stunning. The floor was a pale oak, with expensive rugs and very comfortable-looking furniture dotted around, and with what looked like original paintings on the walls. The dining room was equally impressive with a table and enough chairs to accommodate twenty people. There were various other smaller rooms, a morning room as Thelma described it, a huge walk-in pantry, and a laundry room that was larger than Jazz's kitchen, and that was just for starters.

Eventually, Jazz said, 'I must get on with my work, but thank you for showing me.' She had the report of the meeting yesterday to get on to the computer, plus the other tasks which Zak had listed for her to do.

'But you haven't seen upstairs — '

'It'll have to wait for another day, I'm afraid. I really do have a lot to do.'

By the end of the afternoon, she felt satisfied with what she'd accomplished. She hadn't seen Zak again, which, in a way, was a relief. Embarrassment still burned over the events of last evening. She couldn't imagine what had come over her — well, she could — too many glasses of wine. She'd never been much of a drinker. Alcohol, any sort of alcohol, went to her head altogether too fast and then she had an unfortunate tendency to act quite out of character.

Normally, she limited herself to a single glass. Trying not to think about what had happened, she packed up for the day, calling a quick goodbye to Thelma before going out to her car. It had been snowing again, she noticed, but not enough to make driving home impossible.

Even so, she took things very cautiously, the light covering of snow was starting to freeze, and her car, unlike Zak's Range Rover, performed adequately on icy roads, but that was all. So, she was heartily relieved to reach her driveway safely.

There was more snow on the ground out here and there was a biting wind blowing straight off the sea. Once she was inside, not surprisingly, the first thing she did was light the fire. As she drew the curtains, she could hear something pattering against the window. She looked out. She wasn't sure if it was raining or snowing — a bit of both, maybe? The wind was certainly blowing harder, making the timbers of the house creak alarmingly as draughts found every crack.

Once she'd eaten, she sat close to the fire to read her book and, as a rare treat, poured herself a glass of wine. She glanced up once or twice at the ceiling, but there were no sounds of anything other than the wood doing what it always did. Gradually she began to relax.

It wasn't until she was lying in bed, on the verge of sleep, that she heard what sounded like someone whispering. She was instantly awake, listening. She thought the sound was coming from downstairs somewhere. The trouble was she couldn't distinguish anything, the words were no more than a low, grumbling mutter, and even as she sat up, it stopped.

What was going on? First — footsteps, then piano music; now someone whispering. It couldn't be what it sounded like — it simply couldn't.

Again, she asked herself — had she

dreamt it? Could it have been the wind, whispering softly as it stole through the cracks in the walls, around the windows? Or the rustling of branches; dead leaves, even? There were enough bushes and trees in the lane as well as the garden. Any of those things could sound like someone whispering, it could even be snow gently falling against the glass of the windows.

Eventually, she settled herself down again and tried to sleep, but her efforts were in vain. She lay, for what felt like hours, cowering beneath her duvet, just as she had done as a child, listening, waiting — She must have finally succumbed to exhaustion, though, and slept, because the next thing she knew it was morning and a bright, white light was filtering around the curtains.

The events of the night before returned to her. In the light of day, it all seemed exaggerated and nonsensical. What she'd heard couldn't have been someone whispering, it didn't make sense. It was the wind playing tricks on her.

She climbed from bed, shivering in the early morning chill, and went to the window. She dragged the curtains aside and looked out. It had snowed even more overnight and it now lay, shrouding the garden in a mantle of white, providing an almost unearthly contrast to the periwinkle sky. Everything sparkled and glistened in the early sunshine.

She ran down to the kitchen, eager for the comforting warmth of the Aga. It didn't disappoint, the room was cosy and welcoming. She opened the door that led directly into the back garden and stepped outside. The cold struck her instantly, making her gasp; the snow was crisp beneath her slipper. It had frozen hard. What on earth was the lane going to be like to drive along? Maybe she'd better go and check?

She'd barely had the thought before her telephone rang. She ran inside to the hall and lifted the receiver.

'Jazz?'

It was Zak.

'Is something wrong?' What on earth could he want at this hour? Unless — was he going to sack her after all?

'Are you planning on coming to the house to work?'

'Well, I was going to try — '

'Don't attempt it in your car. I'll come and pick you up. The snow has frozen. There's already been an accident outside the house.'

'I'm sure I'll manage — '

'No. If anything happened to you, I'd feel responsible. I'll be there for nine forty five.' And he was gone again, just like that.

She replaced the receiver again, muttering 'the master has spoken — ' Even so, his concern warmed her. It was good to feel protected, cared for.

Zak was starting to appear, increasingly, the very antithesis to the man whom Joel described. She wondered briefly if they'd had some sort of row in the past which had provoked the hostility that seemed to prevail between them. Of course, they were rivals to buy Cliff House, so she supposed that could be at the root of it.

She'd just poured herself a cup of coffee and begun to eat a slice of toast when the phone rang again.

'Goodness, I'm popular this morning,' she murmured, going to lift the receiver. Unless it was Zak, saying he couldn't fetch her, after all.

'Hello?'

'Jazz?'

Who else did they think it would be? It was her phone, after all, in her house — 'That's me. Hello, Joel.'

'I wondered how you were planning to get to work — presuming you're going in this weather.'

'I am — yes.'

'In that case, I'll pick you up and take you.'

'There's no need, Zak's fetching me.'

'Good God, is he? He must desperately need your services.'

'No, he's just a very thoughtful man,

Joel — ' Silence greeted this statement, ' — as you are, clearly,' she hastened to assure him. She didn't wish to add to the pair's animosity with her careless words. Joel, she was discovering, could be very touchy with regards to Zak. Could it be that they weren't simply business rivals, but had, at one time, also been rivals for a woman's affections? Or had one stolen business from the other in some way? 'Two men worrying about me,' she quipped, 'I mustn't let it go to my head.'

'I'm sure it won't. You must be accustomed to men flocking around you.'

He was making her sound like some sort of Mata Hari, the last person she felt like, sitting as she was in a fairly old dressing gown and slippers.

'You're not disputing that, so it must be true.' His tone now was a strange mix of amusement and disapproval. 'In which case, before Rivers or anyone else beats me to it, I was wondering — would you come out with me this evening for a meal?'

Her spirit lifted, instantly. 'Oh, Joel, I'd love to. It would be just the antidote to a bleak winter evening.' It would also get her out of the house once more. For the truth was — no matter how often she told herself that what she was hearing couldn't be what it sounded like — she was becoming more and more unnerved.

'Good. So I'll pick you up at seven thirty, shall I? If the roads are still icy, it might make for a slow journey. Unless, you feel like a bit of cross country skiing?' he joked.

'I think I'll pass on that, as intriguing as it sounds.'

Jazz replaced the receiver, a smile lifting her lips too. Upon reflection, she quite liked the idea of being thought a woman beautiful enough to have men flocking around her. She laughed out loud at the image that that induced. It was miles away from reality. Oh, she'd had men friends, even the odd lover — one at a time, however, she'd never been a flirt; but not one of them had ever felt like the love of her life. There had been one, though — she'd actually been on the verge of suggesting they move in together when she made the agonising and humiliating discovery that he'd been seeing someone else at the same time. He'd been good looking — too good looking, with bucket loads of charm and charisma. Since then, she'd made it a policy to steer well clear of overly attractive men.

She was ready and waiting when Zak turned up and hooted his car horn from outside. She slithered her way to the vehicle, in spite of having put on a pair of sensible boots. Zak saw her struggling and instantly climbed from the car to go to her assistance.

'You're right. I wouldn't want to drive in this,' she laughed up at him. 'Thank you for coming.'

'My pleasure, I can assure you,' and his eyes darkened as he slid an arm around her and clamped her to his side — thankfully, because almost at once her feet began to slide from beneath her. But for Zak's tight grip, she would almost certainly have fallen.

The journey to his house was a nerve-racking one, despite his four wheel drive car. She would never have made it in her own. Nonetheless, that wasn't the sole reason for the lurching of her heart. The proximity of her employer also played its part.

'I hope this has thawed by this evening,' she said, trying to stop her voice from shaking, as well as introduce a note of normality into the situation.

He slanted a glance at her.

Oh Lord, had he detected her agitation? Apparently not, because all he said was, 'Why? What's happening this evening?'

'Joel's taking me out for a meal.'

His jaw tightened then, causing a muscle to flex in it, as a deep frown tugged at his brow. 'I hope he's planning to use a more suitable vehicle that that bone rattler he usually drives.' His tone was one of disapproval — and something else. Something she couldn't quite put a finger on.

'Oh, I'm sure he's thought of that. He rang too, to offer me a lift to your house — '

'Did he now? You want to be careful of Scott.'

'Oh,' she riposted, 'he said more or less the same about you.'

He slanted another glance at her but didn't say anything. They reached the manor house without further incident or comment.

As she clambered from the Range Rover, Zak said, 'I'll run you home again this afternoon. I've got to go out for a while this morning, but I'll be back in plenty of time.'

It was on the tip of her tongue to ask where he was going, but something in the set of his expression warned her not to. Maybe he was meeting a woman? Sara? The very notion made her heart lurch violently. No, no, no. This wasn't happening. She wasn't falling for Zak Rivers; no way. He was definitely off limits, way out of her league, but, even more importantly, she didn't really trust him.

'Okay, I'll see you then. Thanks for the lift.'

But he didn't reply and within seconds was gone, tyres skidding on the icy surface, their deep treads despatching a shower of glistening particles up behind him.

* * *

Jazz made serious headway that day on the tasks that Zak had set her and by lunchtime, felt she could sit back and relax for a while, instead of working while she ate. As usual, Thelma brought her a tray, ' — unless you'd rather eat it with me in the kitchen?'

Jazz would, so she followed the housekeeper out of the office. A close friendship was developing between the two women, so she didn't feel any embarrassment about asking questions. And Thelma invariably seemed more than ready to satisfy her curiosity.

'Is there a woman in Zak's life?' she asked now, hungrily drinking the homemade soup.

'Not as far as I know at the moment. Of course, there've been lots — as you'd expect. He's so good looking, don't you think?'

She glanced at Jazz expectantly. Jazz gave a deliberately ambiguous smile. Not for anything would she admit she found her employer handsome. Who knew what Thelma might be tempted to tell him in an indiscreet moment?

'He hasn't mentioned anyone in particular lately, though, and, as far as I know, he's not brought anyone back here with him — '

'What about a woman called Sara?'

'Yes, I remember Sara. He was seeing her for quite some time. I — and she, I suspect — thought something might come of that. She was always here — used to act as his hostess for dinner parties. I think a lot of people thought they would settle down together.'

'So — what happened?'

Thelma shrugged, her expression a reflective one. 'Haven't a clue. She suddenly stopped coming, and Zak isn't one who would welcome questions about his private life.'

So, that was that. She was none the wiser about what it was that made Zak tick.

'Do you know Joel Scott?' she decided to ask.

'Joel Scott? Um — oh yes, he works with that Blake Carlisle. Zak has mentioned them now and again. Don't really know anything about him, though. Why?'

'I'm going out with him tonight. He's my next door neighbour. Zak warned me to be careful of him. I wondered why. I knew Joel as a boy, when I used to come and stay with my aunt, but that was a long time ago. People can — and do — change.'

'Well, all I can say is — if Zak warned you about him, take heed. Of course, they are business rivals, so there's bound to be a bit of tension — It does sound as if it might be a little more than that, though.' She shrugged. 'But that's it really. He doesn't discuss his affairs — business or personal — with me. I wish he did.' She flashed a wicked grin. 'It might make things a darn sight more interesting.'

So, for the second time in as many minutes, that was that. She was no further along in her quest for the truth about the hostility between the two men.

* * *

Jazz watched the rain that had begun to fall, washing away the snow. The temperature had risen considerably in the last hour or two — ever since Zak had driven her home. He'd been a bit more talkative, telling her some details about the people he'd been to see that day. Of course, he'd had an ulterior motive in being friendly — as she'd pretty soon discovered.

'I'll leave some rough notes on your desk,' he said, 'so in the morning you can straighten them up; you know — put them into grammatical English and then print them out for me.' He fell silent for a moment, and then said, 'I was wondering if you'd — ' he paused again, his sideways glance a speculative one, 'well, the long and short of it is, I need to hold a dinner party in a week or so — for some business friends and their wives — I owe them.'

Jazz turned her head and looked at him. What on earth was he telling her that for? His entertaining arrangements were nothing to do with her. And she couldn't imagine he'd be asking her to dinner.

'My last PA, Maggie, usually arranged things. You know, invitations if required, or phone calls, she'd plan the menu with Thelma, organise the seating plan, that sort of thing — iron out any problems that arise.'

She'd thought the current girlfriend did that for him — according to

Thelma that was — but, if there wasn't a girlfriend — ?

'What I want to ask you is — will you do the same thing? You'll also attend, naturally — as my hostess, that goes without saying.'

Wow! That was the last thing Jazz had expected to hear. He hadn't mentioned hostess duties when he'd offered her the job.

'It would be for sixteen people,' he went on, 'including you and me, and I was thinking — how does a week this Saturday sound?'

'Yes, I'm sure I can manage that — '

How had she done that? Sounded so calm, so unconcerned, when her mind was reeling with all the force of a whirlwind at the task that lay ahead of her? The most people she'd ever organised supper for were four, and then it had only been for friends, and it had been a takeaway at that. This sounded like a whole different ball-game; the opposite end of the spectrum completely.

'Good. I'll leave you the list of guests, their names and phone numbers for tomorrow. So — I can leave it all to you, then?'

Jazz nodded; she felt quite sick all of a sudden. What the hell had she done, agreeing to something that at the moment seemed way beyond her capabilities? Still, she'd got Thelma. She must have done this sort of thing before — She'd help her.

But that wasn't to be the end of her troubles. Flick rang. 'Can we come down this weekend? I want Gary to see the house.'

What else could she say but, 'Yes, of course. When will you be coming?'

'Early Saturday morning. We'll have to go again on Sunday evening. Gary needs to be at work on the dot on Monday. He has to show willing. They're talking redundancies and as he hasn't been there that long, he could be one of the first to go — unless he can make himself indispensable. Oh, Jazz, if he has to go, I don't know what we'll do. We'll have no money. The redundancy won't be much, he hasn't been there long enough to merit a big pay out.'

Jazz closed her eyes at the sound of her sister's distress, sensing what was coming next. 'Flick, you did use that cheque I gave you to pay some of your debts didn't you? And what happened to the money Emily left you?'

Flick didn't answer straight away and Jazz felt her heart sink.

'It's gone,' she finally admitted, 'swallowed up in repayments. But I have used your cheque to pay off some of the credit cards — although I did keep a bit back. There were things we simply had to have, Jazz.'

'What things, Flick.' She sighed wearily.

'Well, you know — bed linen, new things for the kitchen.' Her voice was starting to rise. 'And we needed a-a new car.'

Jazz gasped. 'You've bought a car?'

'Yeah. We need something reliable,

and the other one was nothing more than trouble. And it's better to pay cash than borrow the money, isn't it? Why do you always have to be so critical of everything I do?' she burst out.

'Okay, okay — sorry.' But Jazz knew in that instant why Flick was planning to visit her. She was going to urge her — no, nag her, pressurise her — to sell Cliff House and then give her half of the money. It was the last thing that Jazz needed to hear at this precise moment. She had a dinner party for sixteen people to organise and the sister from hell was about to visit. No, that was unfair. She loved her sister. It was just that — she sighed — Flick honestly believed that everyone owed her something, Jazz, evidently, most of all.

A horn blasting from outside of the house signalled Joel's arrival. He was early. Still holding the phone to her ear, she opened the door and waved. 'Flick, I have to go — '

'Hey,' Joel greeted her as she climbed into the car. The snow had all but disappeared, leaving slushy puddles in its wake. 'You look great.'

'Thank you.' Her efforts had evidently paid off. She'd devoted quite a lot of thought to what she should wear this evening, and in the end, unsure what sort of restaurant Joel would be taking her to, had plumped for something midway between dressy and casual. So, she was wearing a long skirt and matching jacket, teamed with a cashmere jumper that did wondrous things for her eyes. 'Sorry to keep you waiting. My sister was on the phone. She and her husband are coming to stay this weekend.'

She couldn't see what Joel was wearing to know if she'd made the right choice of clothes or not. His coat was three quarters long and, draped in casual elegance around his neck, was a smart burgundy, navy and grey striped scarf. It looked like silk.

'Great scarf,' she commented. 'I noticed it the other day.'

He touched it — almost tenderly

with one hand. 'My mother gave it to me, not long before she died. I like wearing it. It reminds me of her.' His eyes misted.

Jazz reached over and squeezed his hand. 'You must miss her very much.'

'Yes, I do. I miss them both, my father and her. The house seems so empty — ' His words limped into silence. 'Anyway, mustn't get maudlin. I hope you like Italian food.'

'I love it.' She felt a thrill of anticipation. She hadn't been out on a date for so long. The experience would distract her from the ordeals of what lay ahead over the next few days — hopefully, at any rate.

'Great. The restaurant's one I go to quite often. The food is something really special.'

★ ★ ★

And he was right. The meal was delicious, cooked in an authentic Italian style. The owner, Mario, had only arrived from Italy five years ago and clearly took great pleasure in talking to his customers. Joel was soon laughing loudly, his lingering grief over the death of his parents evidently forgotten — for the moment at least.

With their main courses consumed, Jazz leant back in her seat and said, 'That's it. I couldn't eat another morsel.'

'Not even some genuine Italian ice-cream?' Joel teased her.

He'd been extremely good company, evoking memories of their times together as children. Mind you, it hadn't always been happiness and laughter between them. She'd recently found herself recalling more than one occasion when he'd deliberately startled and frightened her. One memorable time, he'd hidden from her for a good half an hour, reducing her to tears and panic at being abandoned as she'd thought, and then making her scream with terror when he'd leapt out at her from wherever he'd been concealed. Fortunately, maturity had rendered him kind and thoughtful, so she had no need to worry about tricks like that now.

'Oh, go on then, just a small one.'

They lingered over dessert, Jazz eating far more than she'd believed she'd be able to. It wasn't until they were walking back to Joel's car that he asked, 'I've been meaning to ask — have you heard any more footsteps?'

'I've put them down to creaky floorboards and an overactive imagination.' She wasn't sure why she was lying, and to Joel of all people, other than the more she talked about what was happening, the more — real it all began to seem. And that terrified her.

'Are you sure that's all it was? I mean — if you're ever frightened, I'm just along the lane.'

He was eyeing her keenly. It was obvious he didn't believe her.

'I'm fine, Joel — really.'

'Okay — if you say so. How's the job going? I trust Rivers has been behaving himself?'

'It's early days yet, but so far I like it.

I also meant to tell you — you're quite wrong about the reason for his PA leaving. She had family problems — It was nothing to do with Zak's behaviour.'

'Oh, yeah?' he scoffed. His face had lost its expression of good humour. 'Rivers tell you that, then?'

'No, actually it was his housekeeper.'

'Well, she would say that, wouldn't she? She wants to keep her job.'

'Joel, I refuse to discuss this and spoil what, till now, has been a most enjoyable evening. Zak has been a very considerate employer. He hasn't put a foot wrong.'

'It's not his foot I'm worried about,' he muttered blackly.

Jazz disregarded that insinuation. 'When we went to Exeter on Monday — '

He stared at her in astonishment. 'You went to Exeter with him. What the hell for?'

'For a business meeting — it's part of the job, to take notes — '

'Hang on. You said Monday. That was

the day of the heavy snowfall. How did you get there and back?'

'We didn't get back.' She realised she'd said too much the second she saw the expression upon Joel's face. It changed from astonished exasperation to indignant outrage.

'You didn't get back?' he echoed. 'So what did you do, for heaven's sake? Sleep in the car?'

'He'd reserved rooms in a hotel — just in case.'

'Just in case of what?' His look, as well as his tone, was heavy with condemnation. 'In case he decided to — '

'Joel,' she all but shouted his name now. 'Stop it. He behaved with impeccable courtesy. There was never any suggestion — ' She felt her face redden as memories of her own behaviour returned to her. If Zak was the sort of man that Joel was insinuating, then things would have ended very differently. Of course, Joel had noticed her expression. 'Something did happen, didn't it? Tell me — '

12

When she didn't respond, Joel grabbed her by her arms and pulled her close. He then lowered his head to hers and started to kiss her, his mouth grinding over hers, roughly, brutally almost.

'Joel,' she finally managed to free herself, 'please — don't.'

The revulsion she felt at his mouth on hers had surprised her. So much so, that once he stopped kissing her, she only just stopped herself from rubbing the feel of him away.

To his credit, however, he released her instantly; so instantly, in fact, that she staggered backwards and almost fell on the slippery tarmac.

'Oh, Jazz — I'm so sorry.' He rubbed a hand over his face, as if by doing that, he could remove all memory of what had just happened. 'I don't know what came over me.'

But Jazz did. 'You're jealous — of Zak Rivers. Why? What's he done?'

'Oh, you mean other than always trying to scupper my and Blake's plans?'

'B-but that's just business, surely; healthy competition?'

'He's deliberately alienated people against us.'

'How can you be sure of that?'

'We lost two sites that we were interested in. He told both people concerned with selling them that Blake was on the verge of bankruptcy and would most likely renege on the deal.'

Jazz was aware of a stirring of unease. Would Zak be capable of such underhand tactics? Or maybe he knew something that Joel didn't? 'And is he — on the verge of bankruptcy?'

'No,' Joel hotly repudiated the suggestion, 'it's just Rivers' way of getting the sites for himself — spreading deliberately misleading rumours. You want to watch him. That man would be capable of anything to make sure he gets what he wants.'

'I'm sure you're wrong, Joel.' But her words sounded unconvincing — even to her. After all, how did she know Joel was wrong? She had no real way of knowing how far Zak would go. He was ruthless, she'd glimpsed that side of him herself, and if Joel was right, he'd lied about a competitor for his own gain. Joel's words resurrected her feelings of unease. If he had done as Joel was accusing, what would he be capable of in his determination to buy her house? Capable of employing her, treating her well — even flirting mildly with her, but then, working secretly to try and frighten her out of Cliff House?

But how would he have gained access to the house? Had the key copied? It had been standing empty for quite a while after Emily's death — and look how he'd been standing in the garden that day. He could have been up to anything. And Emily had had a dreadful habit of leaving a door key hidden beneath a stone by the back door.

Jazz hadn't discovered that fact until a few days after she'd moved in, when she'd been tidying up the garden and had moved the stone. But if he was responsible for the sounds she'd been hearing at night, how would he do it? Did he let himself in, do whatever he needed to, like walk across a bedroom floor, turn on the radio, then the second he heard her moving about, leave as silently as he'd entered? But how would he do that without her spotting him? And she'd never once found any evidence of someone having been there. But he'd make sure that he left no physical evidence behind him, wouldn't he? Otherwise, there'd be no point, not if his aim was to scare her into selling.

She shivered. If any of this was true, then she was working for a monster; a monster who had no qualms about cheating his rivals out of business contracts, or about frightening a defenceless woman.

No, the truth was she simply couldn't believe that a man like Zak Rivers, powerful, wealthy, a highly successful man, would go to the extreme lengths of terrifying a woman — just to get his hands on her house. And she still wasn't entirely sure that it wasn't all down to extremely realistic dreams.

'I can't believe — ' she began.

Joel snorted. 'Oh, take it from me, believe it — I've known Rivers a lot longer than you, and there's nothing that that man wouldn't stoop to in his endless pursuit of wealth and power.'

Their journey home was a more subdued one than the outward one had been. Jazz tried several times to get the conversation started, but she was unsuccessful. Joel had closed himself off from her and that saddened her. She needed all the friends she could get.

When they reached Cliff House, in a last ditch attempt to repair things between them, she said with genuine warmth, 'Thank you, Joel, I've had a great evening — '

'You're welcome. Look, I have to go — I'll talk to you again.'

He made no move to kiss her again; it was as if he couldn't wait to get away. She'd let a couple of days pass and then go and talk to him, try and put things right between them. She didn't want to leave things like this: cold, unfriendly; hostile, even. He was her nearest neighbour, as well as a good friend.

She was in the bedroom, preparing herself for bed, when the music started. And this time, there was no mistake. She was wide awake and still dressed — well, partially, at any rate. She pulled on her discarded sweater, then, taking hold of the cricket bat which she now kept propped up by the bed, headed for the stairs. Slowly, soundlessly, she started down them. The music was definitely coming from the dining room. Someone must be in there, playing the piano? There was no other rational explanation. She didn't allow herself to explore the possibilities of the irrational. If she did that, she'd lose her nerve and probably hightail it back to the bedroom, and she was determined to uncover the truth this time. Could it be Zak? Or was it someone — or something — else? She needed to know, even if it did turn out to be something supernatural.

A pulse pounded in her throat as she crossed the hallway towards the dining room doorway. She reached the threshold at the exact moment that the music stopped. Determined, despite the upsurge of fear, to take on whoever — or whatever — was in there, she lifted the cricket bat into the air and walked into the room.

It was empty. There was no-one there, and no more music. The piano lid was closed.

Yet the notes had sounded so real. Oh God! Could she be losing her mind? Hearing things that weren't there? Could she have developed some form of schizophrenia? That led you to believe you were hearing things, didn't it: voices; music even? She listened again, not daring to breathe, not moving, but, it was to no avail, she couldn't hear anything at all.

She sank down onto the piano stool, and, dropping the bat, put both hands to her face. With no evidence of a flesh and blood intruder — could it really be that the house was haunted? No, she didn't believe in ghosts. She repeated the words, over and over — as if that would remove any possibility of such a thing.

Yet, she was hearing something, of that she was certain. Thank goodness Flick was coming at the weekend. For all that her sister was intensely exasperating, right now she was looking like a positive haven of security — because if Flick heard the sounds too, then Jazz would know it wasn't something that only she could hear. It wasn't just in her head.

Knowing she'd be unable to sleep after this, Jazz went to the kitchen and made herself a hot drink. As she sipped it, for the first time, she asked herself — should she sell Cliff House? Give everyone what they wanted, and more importantly, give herself peace of mind.

She returned to bed eventually but still found sleep impossible. She lay, allowing herself to relax, inch by inch, until finally sleep overtook her. But it proved a fitful sleep, punctuated with vivid dreams. Emily was there, calling her at one point. 'Jazz, where am I? See if you can find me?' And Jazz was a child again, searching every corner, every possible hiding place, finding nothing but driven on by Emily's voice. She woke in the end crying, 'I can't find you. Where are you?' Her legs were tangled in the duvet, a pillow was on the floor, and she was sweating profusely, strands of hair sticking to her scalp. She opened her eyes and there was Emily, as clear as if she were actually in the room with her. Jazz was suddenly overwhelmed with a deep sense of loss as her aunt's final words echoed in her head. 'Be careful, darling — be careful. Don't get lost — '

Jazz sat up. Dream or not, Emily had been warning her — but of what?

Could her aunt have been experiencing the same torment that she was — as she'd wondered once before — but had feared telling anyone, even Beth, for fear of being branded a lunatic?

Oh no, please don't let it be that. Yet Emily had died looking frightened. Beth had told her that. Had someone — something — literally scared her to death? Jazz covered her eyes with her hand and whispered, 'I'll find out, Emily. I'll uncover the truth — whatever it is.'

★ ★ ★

The following morning she rang Zak to say she needed the day off — personal business, she told him.

He immediately agreed, which meant Jazz could set off for the town, for the library, to be exact. The morning was a crisply cold one but she decided to walk, even though the library was on the far side of the town. People greeted her, smiling, visibly pleased to see her. Her spirits rose. St. Kernan had begun to feel well and truly like home.

The library, when she reached it, had a surprisingly extensive reference section, considering its limited size. A search along the shelves quickly unearthed several history books of the sort she was looking for. She was hoping they would provide facts about a few of the town's older houses and their occupants, in particular, Cliff House, as well as details of the area as a whole.

She pulled them from the shelf and carried them to a table set in front of a window. An elderly man was already sitting there, leafing through the local paper.

'Morning,' he said. 'Looks like a fair ole bit of reading you've got there.'

Jazz eyed the pile of books. 'It does, doesn't it? I may have been a little ambitious. It'll take me all day to go through them.'

'Aren't you from Cliff House — ' His

eyes glinted with curiosity, ' — Emily's place?'

'Yes, I'm her niece.'

'So — how are you liking it out there? Bit lonely I'd have thought — for a young un' like you.'

'It can be. I'm getting used to it, though. I take it you knew Emily?'

'Oh yes. We all know each other hereabouts. She used to come in here — well, when she had time. She loved her history did Emily. The last time I saw her she had a pile of books — just like you. Said she was researching the previous owners of her house.'

'Did she? That's what I'm about to do. Um — how long was that before she died?'

'Ooh, now — let's see. No more'n a week or two, I wouldn't have thought.'

Something struck Jazz then. Here was someone who, from the sound of it, had lived locally for years. Who better to tell her about Cliff House?

'I don't suppose you could tell me a bit about the house. You know — who's lived there over the centuries, things like that. Who died there? There must be loads of unusual and interesting things that have happened.'

'Well, I was a member of the local history society for a while and they uncovered a few tales I can tell you.'

'I'd love to hear whatever you know.'

'Okay. Well, as you probably know, the house is some three hundred years old and some very strange things are supposed to have happened in that time. Don't know whether they're true, of course, they could just be fairy tales.' His gaze sharpened. 'Why, has something happened out there?'

'Please — go on.'

'Well, as I said, it's only stories passed down through the generations; I don't think anything's documented. Okay, now let me see — there was one young woman according to local rumour — oh, about a hundred and fifty years ago — her husband was thought to have poisoned her. Then there was some fella' found dead with a knife in his gut. It was suspected one of his friends had done for him. He'd been messing about with the friend's wife. That was towards the end of the nineteenth century. He was some sort of musician, I think — '

'What did he play? Was it a piano by any chance?'

'Dunno. Just know he was a musician — hang on, yes, it could have been a piano. It rings a bell.' He eyed her keenly. 'Why do you want to know all this stuff, anyway? Are you sure nuthin's happened?'

None of what he was saying was making her feel any better, because if it had been a piano — ? Maybe she shouldn't have started this?

'Nothing's happened.' She couldn't tell him what she'd been hearing. Knowing old people, the likelihood was it would be all over the town by this evening, and that was the last thing she wanted — to be known as 'the crazy woman at Cliff House who's hearing piano music in the middle of the night — '.

'Well — if you want more — a baby was found dead in his cot. Foul play was suspected. It was thought his mother smothered him. That's it really. All I know at any rate. I doubt if those books of yours will tell you anything — as I said, it's all hearsay.'

'Well, thank you, anyway. You've been very helpful — '

The old man got to his feet. 'I'll leave you to it then — '

'Um — you didn't tell me your name,' Jazz said.

'Bill — Bill Chapman — '

Despite minutely examining the books she'd found, Jazz couldn't find any mention of unexplained deaths or mysterious happenings in the house. Bill had been right; nothing was written down. He couldn't have made it all up, could he? There'd been a definite twinkle in his eye. But surely he wouldn't do that, knowing it would most likely frighten her?

She decided to call on Beth and see if she could corroborate Bill's stories.

Fortunately, her friend was at home and extremely pleased to see her.

'I met a man called Bill Chapman,' Jazz began, 'in the library. I was trying to find out a bit more about the history of Cliff House and its occupants. He had a load of stories — '

'Oh yes. And what's he been filling your head with? That man should write a book. The Brothers Grimm would be mild in comparison. He loves scaring folk. Take it all with a pinch of salt — '

'H-he told me about a musician who died in suspicious circumstances. He might have been a pianist. He also said Emily had been researching the history of the house just before she died. Did she say anything to you — tell you what she was looking for?'

'No, she didn't. You don't believe it's him that you've heard?'

'We-ell, it does seem a bit of a coincidence. I'm hearing piano music and he's a pianist . . . '

'Jazz, if you're thinking it's a ghost you've been hearing — well, I don't want to be rude but I've never heard such nonsense. You were dreaming, my love.'

Not last night she hadn't been. But she wasn't about to tell Beth that. Not yet. Her friend might begin to doubt her sanity, as she herself had started to do.

'You forget all that Bill said. He's a wicked old mischief maker in my opinion.'

* * *

But that proved easier said than done. Work helped, especially with the dinner party to arrange.

She consulted extensively with Thelma on the menu and, then there were the phone calls to the prospective guests. They all eagerly accepted Jazz's invitation, with more than one woman subjecting her to a barrage of questions about her relationship to Zak. She very swiftly made it clear she was phoning them as part of her job as his PA. She didn't want any embarrassing misunderstandings to arise.

The flower arrangements that were to be placed around the house and on the dining room table were ordered for delivery on the morning of the dinner, and last, but not least, she began to work on the seating plan. That proved the biggest stumbling block of all; she'd never, after all, met any of the guests, and one misplacement could mean disaster if they didn't get on for some reason.

And she had to do all of this as well as her usual work, so she was kept frantically busy. All of which meant, she was heartily glad when Friday night arrived and she could concentrate on the relatively simple task of preparing for Flick and Gary's arrival.

But the weekend didn't provide the break she'd hoped for.

From the moment she arrived, Flick subjected her to a more or less continual harangue about the house.

Gary, as they had feared, had indeed been made redundant, and his pay off wasn't brilliant.

'We're completely broke,' Flick repeatedly wailed. 'You'll have to sell Cliff House; it's the only way —'

This, of course, only made Jazz all the more determined not to — despite what was going on at night. She'd always hated conceding defeat over anything, and selling her home would, in her eyes, be the greatest defeat of all. To hand over her aunt's cherished house to a property developer.

She'd debated telling Flick what was happening, but in the end decided not to. It would only give her sister more reason to urge her to sell. And as it happened, there were no unexplained sounds of any sort, so she had no excuse to bring it up anyway. No — whatever was happening was happening just to her. And that conclusion wasn't the one she had wished to reach.

By the time Sunday evening came, Jazz was heartily relieved to wave Flick and Gary off. They departed with another large cheque. It had been the only way to get Flick off her back. And she didn't want to see her sister destitute, in any case. When Jazz had tried to suggest they curtail their spending for a while and Flick had angrily retaliated with, 'Oh well, it's easy for you to say that. You're all right. Aunt Emily made sure of that — Don't you think it's all just a bit unfair?' Jazz had abandoned the argument. Flick was only interested in herself — as much as Jazz hated to think it. Her sister had asked no real questions about Jazz and her life in St. Kernan, so Jazz had responded by saying very little about anything.

* * *

It was the following night that things started again. Jazz was once again woken by the sounds of the piano being played. Bill's tale of the musician who'd died had been echoing repeatedly in her head, so the notion of it all being down to a restless spirit wasn't sounding quite so improbable. What should she do? Ignore the sounds or get up and investigate? But really, what was the point? She didn't ever find anything.

For the first time then, she wondered if it could be her aunt. Emily had been an accomplished pianist and was already appearing to her in dreams — or, at least, she thought she'd been dreaming. But what if she hadn't been? What if her aunt was trying to warn her of something? But that didn't explain the footsteps, and the whispering. What would be the purpose of them? And the more she thought about it, the more she doubted that Emily would deliberately set about frightening her.

So, yet again, she picked up the cricket bat and began to make her way downstairs. She was halfway down when the music stopped and she saw a beam of light blazing across the hallway from the kitchen.

Someone was in the house, someone

who would need the lights on to see — because she was positive that she'd turned them off before going to bed. She hadn't even bothered to switch them all on. Anyway, it definitely ruled out the possibility of the intruder being a ghost. Ghosts didn't need lights. She didn't know whether to be relieved or alarmed by that.

She grasped the bat tightly in both hands, fully prepared to use it. She was at the foot of the stairs when she heard a voice. A man's voice and it was coming from the kitchen.

Her heart hammered as she crept forwards. The lights still blazed and someone continued to talk, although she couldn't make out the actual words. Her mouth was so dry by this time it was hurting. She tried to swallow, to moisten it, but couldn't. She inched towards the open door and stopped again, listening.

She never knew afterwards how she managed to do it, but she went into the kitchen. Of course, just like the other times, there was no-one there. The voice was coming from the radio. It was some sort of news programme. She dropped the bat with a loud clatter and was running towards the radio, intending to switch it off when she saw it.

Hell, she couldn't miss it. The writing was on the window, neatly printed, the crimson letters six inches high. WHY DON'T YOU GO — GO — GO —

Her feet felt frozen to the floor; even her breathing stopped. Someone had been here, in the house, in this room.

She switched the radio off and as she did so she heard a click. Someone was still here — Without giving herself time to lose her nerve, she dashed into the hall.

'Okay,' she shouted, swinging the bat in front of her to show she meant business, 'whoever you are — show yourself. The game's over.'

No-one answered. She swivelled on her heels, looking wildly around; there was no-one there, and no sign of anyone having been there. She hurried into the dining room and snapped on the light. That room too was empty. The piano lid was down; all was exactly as it should be.

This was no ghost. That click she'd just heard could have been the front door closing as someone went out. She rushed back into the hall and yanked the front door open. She peered out into the darkness and saw — nothing. If someone had been inside the house, they'd managed to get out again and disappear almost instantly.

The implications of this paralysed her with fright. Someone had access to her house to do whatever they wanted, whenever they wanted. Anything could happen. Why — she could be murdered in her bed — as she slept. She moaned softly. She couldn't stay here; she'd pack a bag and leave, right now, simply get into her car and drive away.

But something, a resolve not to be beaten, not to be driven away, filled her. And if they'd intended harming her

— physically — surely they'd have done it by now? It had to be a bluff, hoping she'd be so terrified, she'd run away. Well, they were going to be disappointed. She'd stay and see this through; she'd find out who was doing this to her and then she'd take whatever steps were needed to stop it. For now, she was going to go on as normal, no matter how hard that might be.

Eventually, she returned to bed, after she cleaned the writing off the kitchen window. She wrapped the duvet tightly around herself, as if by so doing, she was gaining some sort of protection. She then lay awake until exhaustion took over and she slept deeply until suddenly, Emily was standing at the foot of her bed, hands outstretched to her niece, her mouth moving, her expression anguished, as she tried to tell Jazz something.

'What?' Jazz shouted. 'Tell me. What's happening? What's wrong?'

But Emily didn't speak, couldn't speak, maybe? And gradually her image faded and disappeared. Jazz awoke with a start and saw that day had broken. Another night was over.

★   ★   ★

It was that evening that Joel turned up at her door, a very repentant-looking Joel, it had to be said. As usual, he had his cherished scarf over his shoulders and was nervously playing with the fringed ends.

Jazz stared hard at him, wondering if it could have been him behind the night-time's events, searching for any sign of guilt. But all she detected was uncertainty; embarrassment. And she really couldn't imagine Joel trying to frighten anyone, let alone her, his childhood playmate.

'Jazz, I'm sorry — really, really sorry. For God's sake, all I seem to do is apologise to you.'

'Come in, Joel. It's too cold to stand on the doorstep.' And it was, a biting wind was blowing straight off the sea, and Jazz thought she could feel the sting of sleet.

'Are you sure?'

'Yes.'

She led the way into the sitting room, where as usual the fire was roaring halfway up the chimney.

'My behaviour was atrocious. I realise that — and then to sulk — ' he grinned ruefully, ' — will you forgive me? I don't want it to affect our friendship.'

'It won't, but,' she eyed him cautiously, 'that's all it is, Joel, friendship. I want you to know that.'

He said nothing for a long moment. 'It's Rivers that you're interested in, isn't it?'

'No, it's not. I work for Zak and that's all — really. And, anyway, he's not my type.'

If only that were true, she told herself once Joel had left again. But the fact was, she was becoming increasingly attracted to her employer, despite her efforts not to be. It didn't help that she saw him practically every day. They'd even spent a lot of that morning together. She'd asked for his help with the seating plan for the dinner party.

But something else had been bothering her. 'Um — you say I will be attending, but I don't want to intrude, push myself forward.'

'You won't be. As I said, you'll be there in the capacity of my hostess for the evening. Um — there's something I've been meaning to mention to you, you'll need some extra money this month — '

'Why?'

'For a new dress, to have your hair done if you like — things like that. As it's part of your job as my PA, I don't expect you to foot the bill.'

'Oh!' Those weren't the sentiments of a man obsessed with wealth and power, or someone intent on terrorising a woman. 'Well, now that you mention it, I don't have anything suitable to wear.' She hadn't actually given that side of things any thought at all. She didn't go in for evening wear. Thank heavens he'd thought of it, otherwise who knew what she'd have had to turn up in? 'But, really, I don't expect you to — '

He'd ignored her protests and whipped out an envelope. He thrust it at her. 'This should take care of it all. There are some very good dress shops in Truro — or so I've been reliably informed.'

Had Sara told him that? 'Thank you.'

'Get something glamorous. I'm sure the other women will pull all the stops out — not that you wouldn't look good in rags, Jazz,' he grinned ruefully at her, clearly aware that he might have been less than tactful in his insinuation that she might not look as good as the other female guests, 'you would, I'm sure. And, of course, you'll stay the night. It'll be too late to drive home alone.'

Her eyes widened. Surely he didn't mean — ?

Amusement gleamed at her from his eyes. Oh Lord, how embarrassing. He knew what she was wondering.

'I'll get Thelma to make up a room for you.'

13

So Jazz did as Zak suggested and went to Truro. She'd been intending to visit ever since she'd arrived in St. Kernan, recalling a visit she'd made as a child with Emily. They'd explored the cathedral, but other than that her mind was a blank. So she was pleased to discover a city full of good shops, meaning that she was ridiculously spoilt for choice. Eventually, she discovered a small boutique where the manageress helped her choose the perfect dress.

As Zak had been more than generous with money, cost wasn't an issue, which was just as well because she opted for a gown in amber and pale lemon chiffon, with a boat-shaped neckline and a flowing skirt that reached down to just above her ankles, and that cost considerably more than she'd ever paid for a dress before — as did the matching shoes and small, clutch bag.

With her purchases made and, confident that she'd done the best she could to hold her own with the women who would doubtlessly have forked out ten times what she had for their outfits, she decided to return home. She hoped that Zak would approve of her choices — after all, he'd paid for it all. She still didn't feel really comfortable with that, especially as he already paid her what she considered an exorbitant salary for what amounted to a part-time job.

She was retracing her steps to her car when she passed a small, brightly lit cafe. She glanced through the window, and was contemplating going in and treating herself to a cup of tea and a slice of cake, when she noticed a couple sitting on the far side of the room.

It was Zak and a woman, Sara; they were leaning in towards each other, talking intently, their hands clasped on the table top between them, their faces mere inches apart. Suddenly, Zak lifted one of Sara's hands to his mouth and kissed her fingers. It was a tender gesture, full of what looked like love.

Jazz pulled back. She didn't want them to catch her watching through the window. It might look as if she were spying on them —

She hurried away, wondering what they'd been talking about so intently. They looked very close still. Maybe they'd been saying goodbye — permanently? Yet, something about them suggested otherwise. And Sara had looked as if she were still keen on Zak when they'd been at Beth's party — Was she trying to resurrect their romance? The idea of that disturbed Jazz — which was ridiculous. As she'd told herself more than once, Zak Rivers was the very last man she should have feelings for. You needed to trust someone for that. Maybe Beth would know what was going on. It was worth asking her. She'd call and see her. It was more than time that she visited; she'd been neglecting her, she'd been so busy.

It was just over an hour later that she was standing in front of Beth's house. All the lights were blazing inside so her friend must be in. Jazz pressed her finger on the bell and waited. The door sprang open almost at once and Beth cried, 'Jazz, how lovely. Come in, dear. I've just put the kettle on.'

'Great, just what I need.'

'So — how's the job going?' Beth hastened about the kitchen, setting out cups and saucers, a plate of biscuits, milk, and sugar. 'I've been wondering.'

'I'm sorry. I should have phoned you.'

'I'm sure you've been busy.'

That was Jazz's cue to tell Beth all about the forthcoming dinner party on Saturday, and her role in it all.

'Well, Zak must trust you then. But — ' she frowned, 'you look — anxious, dear. Is everything all right?'

'I think so. It's proving a bit stressful, to be honest. I've never arranged a dinner party before for sixteen people.

Four is the most I've cooked for.'

Beth looked at her in astonishment. 'You're not doing the cooking, surely?'

Jazz gave a crack of laughter. 'Thank goodness, no. Thelma's doing that.'

'Well, then, a resourceful girl like you. You'll manage.'

'I hope you're right. Um, Beth — ' She hesitated then. Should she even be mentioning this to Beth? Would she be breaking a confidence? 'I've just come from Truro — '

'No work today then?' Beth began pouring the tea.

'No. Zak gave me the day off — to go and buy a new dress for Saturday.'

'That's nice of him. He can be very thoughtful, can't he? I knew all the rumours about him couldn't be true.'

'Wh-what rumours?'

'Oh, you know — that he's only interested in making money, got no time for people, that sort of thing — a heartless womaniser.'

'Oh, I see. Yes — well — '
Again, she hesitated.

'What's wrong, Jazz? Did you not find a dress, is that it?'

'No, I found one.'

'So, what is it then?'

'As I was walking back to where I'd parked the car, I passed a cafe — '

Beth was looking more than a little confused by this time. 'Yes? They do have them in Truro. Several, I believe,' and she winked, good-humouredly.

'I saw — I saw Zak.'

'So?' Beth shrugged.

'He was with Sara. They were holding hands across the table, and — well, he kissed her hand and I was wondering — '

'What?' Beth took a mouthful of tea.

'Are they together again?'

Beth put her cup down and gazed, somewhat uncertainly, at Jazz. 'I'm not sure if I should tell you this — seeing as you work for him now — but I saw Sara's mum a couple of days ago and she said she wouldn't be surprised if they were getting back together — and well, Sara has just broken up with someone else. Jenny — that's Sara's mum — thinks she's never really got over Zak, and she knows they've been meeting.' Beth suddenly looked worried; agitated. 'Don't repeat that, though. Promise me you won't mention what I've just said to Zak. He'd be furious, I'm sure, to think anyone was talking about him; speculating, you know. I believe he's a very private man.'

'I won't say anything.'

'Although, it does seem strange that he's asked you to be his hostess. If he and Sara were back on, surely he'd have asked her? Or maybe he did, and she couldn't do it at such short notice?' She regarded Jazz, a frown tugging at her brow. 'Jazz, are you okay?'

Jazz nodded. 'Yes, I'm fine.'

'You haven't — ?'

'What?'

'Well, got involved with him, have you?'

'No, I'm not involved with him — not in the way that you mean. Look — I must go. Thanks for the tea, Beth.'

But she wasn't fine, she admitted to herself. For no matter what she told herself, she was becoming more and more attracted to Zak, and what Beth had just told had not been what she'd wanted to hear.

Jazz walked back to her car and got in. Beth's words had given her plenty to think about and, after all, Jazz had seen them with her own eyes. It was all too evident there was something unfinished between the pair.

'Jazz.' Someone was tapping on the car window.

It was Joel. He opened the car door and leant in. 'Are you all right? You were deep in thought then.'

'I'm fine.' She wished people would stop asking her that.

'Sure?'

No, she wasn't, and she experienced a sudden longing to confide in him, especially when he walked around to the other side of the car and climbed into the passenger seat. 'You can tell me, you know. Is it Rivers — is he still pestering you — to sell Cliff House?'

But she couldn't say anything. She'd told Beth she wouldn't. And, in any case, Joel was the last person she should confide in, knowing how he felt about her. He was already jealous of Zak. Sharing her growing feelings would simply exacerbate that.

So instead she asked, 'No. Do you want a lift home? I'm going back now.'

'Not going back to work then?'

'No, I've got the day off.'

'Oh? How come? I heard that Rivers is a hard task master.'

'Who told you that?'

'I can't remember.'

'More gossip, Joel?' she riposted. 'You really shouldn't listen to such talk. It isn't even true and I should know. Now, do you want that lift home?'

* * *

Once she was home again, she found she couldn't settle to anything. She wandered around the house, picking up things, putting them down again, restless and unhappy. Her future stretched out bleakly in front of her; a solitary existence with no-one to care for, or to care for her.

Oh, get over yourself. You've got Joel, Beth — She went into the kitchen to find the materials to make a start on cleaning up after Flick and Gary. That would take her mind off things. Her sister and husband weren't the tidiest of couples, so it took a few hours of strenuous work. By the time she'd finished, she was tired enough to drop into a chair by the fire and close her eyes.

She must have dozed off because suddenly she was jumping awake to the sound of someone banging on the front door. Now what? Who could it be? It was gone nine o'clock. Unease quivered through her, so it was with a great deal of caution that she opened the door — to see her sister standing there.

'Flick, why are you here and so soon

again?' Surely she couldn't be back for more money?

'Thank God. I was beginning to think you were out and I've come all this way. I had to see you.' She began to weep. 'You have to help me; I'm in so much debt. I can't tell Gary, he'll go completely insane.'

'Come in then.'

Flick followed her into the lounge. They're threatening to cut off the electricity, the phone, the gas bill's due . . . '

'Oh, Flick,' Jazz sighed.

'Five grand would see us straight.'

Jazz's heart sank. 'I've already given you a very substantial amount, Flick.'

'I know, but, please, one last time.'

'Okay, but I can't keep forking out. I've got the upkeep of this house to consider.'

'Well, if you'd sell it, there'd be no problem.'

'I'm not going to discuss that again. Emily wanted me to have it. She'd promised me that one day I'd live in it, and that's what I'm going to do. I'd feel I was letting her down by selling it.'

Fortunately, Flick was soon pleading tiredness and took herself off to bed. Jazz decided to do the same. It was as she was walking past Flick's bedroom that she heard her sister on her mobile phone. She didn't mean to eavesdrop but she couldn't help overhearing her sister's words.

' — she's weakening. I can hear it in her voice. If we carry on — '

Her voice dropped too low then to hear anymore. Jazz walked slowly to her own room. Carry on — what? What were her sister and her husband up to? It must have been Gary she was talking to. The thought flashed into her head. Oh no. It couldn't be Gary and Flick responsible for what was happening to her, could it? They were very keen for her to sell. But — Flick wouldn't do that, surely?

Jazz's head began to spin. No — in any case, how would they manage it? They lived miles away. And Flick didn't have a key. She could have had one cut, though, a tiny voice whispered. Jazz had taken the key back to the Midlands with her. It had been hanging on a hook in the kitchen for a while. And looked at logically, Flick and Gary wouldn't even have to come here — not if they had an accomplice in St. Kernan; an accomplice who was also desperate for Jazz to sell. And Flick knew that Zak was keen to buy the house. She could have approached him, given him a key, and, knowing how Jazz's imagination worked, suggested that frightening her out of her wits would be a good way of persuading her to sell. It would suit both parties. Zak would get the house and Flick would hopefully get half the money. In fact, it could even have been Zak she was talking to.

No, Flick wouldn't subject her to such-such torment, Jazz told herself — unless she was really desperate — which of course she was.

She should ask Flick, demand to know the truth, but her nerve failed her. If she was wrong, it would permanently damage relations between the two of them, and she wasn't prepared to do that — not without some proof.

Flick left the next morning, Jazz could only assume she'd got what she'd come for so there was no point in staying. For the first time then, she felt real dislike for her older sister. She was being used, and if her suspicions had any foundation to them at all, betrayed in the worst possible way.

*   *   *

And as if all that weren't enough, that evening she was disturbed once again by something banging, not on the door this time but somewhere outside of the house. She went to the front door and opened it, not fully, just wide enough to peer through the gap.

The wind had risen and was blowing fiercely. She stepped outside. It was raining — hard. She glanced around.

The garage doors were standing open, banging back and forth, and the interior light was on.

Jazz frowned. She didn't make a habit of locking them, but she was sure she'd closed them. But then again, maybe she hadn't. She was so upset, so distracted by all that was happening to her that she didn't know what she was doing half the time. But had she turned the light on? She couldn't remember.

Hunching her shoulders against the rain, she made a dash for the garage, intending to simply close the doors and run back into the house. That was until she saw the rubbish just inside the entrance. A large pile of tin cans, bottles, polystyrene cups, vegetable peelings — all things that she knew she hadn't put there, and couldn't possibly have fallen out of the dustbin; that was on the opposite side of the driveway, just around the side of the house, yards away.

She stood, rooted to the spot, oblivious to the rain plastering her hair to her head and soaking her clothes, with her heart pounding so fast it made her feel sick. This had been done deliberately. Someone had come here and dumped their garbage. Why? But more to the point, who? And were they still here, hiding, waiting to see what her reaction would be? Taking malicious pleasure in it? Well, she wasn't going to give it to them. She slammed the garage doors shut on it all, she'd clear it in the morning. She darted another glance around and then ran back inside.

Yet again, that night Jazz laid awake, turning endless possibilities over and over in her mind, straining to hear the least sound, inside the house or out of it. It didn't help that the wind had reached gale force and was hurling itself against the walls of the house. It meant that floorboards creaked, and draughts squealed through every minuscule gap, rattling window frames, shaking doors — She lay, stiff, every nerve end jangling, until, eventually, she gave up trying to sleep and went downstairs.

What was she going to do? She

couldn't accuse anyone, not without some evidence, some proof of wrongdoing. And she had none, not one shred. Again, whoever it was had been far too clever to leave any sort of evidence behind them.

For the second time, she wondered about Flick's involvement. Could whoever had done this tonight been the person she'd been phoning last night?

But the onset of dawn brought an even firmer determination to stay put, not to surrender to such cruel persecution, because that's what it was — persecution, pure and simple. She'd go and clear up the mess outside and then go to work; carry on as normal. It was the only thing to do.

So that's what she did, and just as she'd hoped, work left no room for anything else. Not even the suspicion that the perpetrator might be Zak.

But then something else happened, something that would make her seriously reconsider her decision to remain in St. Kernan.

She was in bed, immersed in a particularly gripping novel when she heard sounds of banging once more. This time it seemed to be coming from inside the house. For God's sake, how much more of this could she take and stay sane?

Buoyed up by fury rather than fear, she ran heedlessly down the stairs to find, just as before, the kitchen lights blazing and one of the windows wide open. It was banging back and forth in the wind, astonishingly still unbroken.

But if the glass had remained intact, Jazz certainly hadn't. Something snapped in that moment, something that had become increasingly fragile with each event that happened and she started to scream, 'Leave me alone — whoever you are. I'm not leaving this house. It's mine — do you hear me?' and she crossed to the open window and slammed it shut.

At the exact same moment, a loud knocking began on the front door. She glanced up at the kitchen clock; it was five minutes to twelve. Who would call at this time, unless they had sinister motives? Her heart began to pound. She'd ignore it, and maybe they'd go away again.

But a second knock sounded, louder and more prolonged this time, right before the bell began to ring in a series of staccato bursts. She'd have to answer it before whoever it was broke down the door. She went into the hallway and opened the door an inch or so. It was Zak. Instinctively, she pulled her dressing gown tighter and said, 'It's you.'

What was he doing here — this late?

'Are you okay? Only I was passing and noticed your lights were all on — '

Passing? Why on earth would he be passing her house at this time of night? Maybe it hadn't been altogether wise to open the door?

' — so I stopped. I've been to visit a friend and was taking a short cut home. Then I thought I heard you screaming — '

'Oh,' Jazz gave what she hoped was a

nonchalant laugh, because if he was the one responsible for everything — and she desperately hoped he wasn't — with or without Flick's collusion, she wasn't about to give him the satisfaction of hearing her admit her fear, 'it must have been the television. I'd mistakenly left it on when I went to bed. I'd only just heard it myself — well, heard the screaming. I came down and switched it off — Sorry.'

'Are you sure that's all it was? You look a bit shaken — '

'It woke me and for a moment I was startled.'

He moved his head and glanced beyond her. 'There's no-one else here then — Scott, for instance?'

'Why on earth would Joel be here?'

He shrugged. 'Why indeed? Well, if you're okay, I'll get off. I can see you're ready for bed,' his glance slid over her, all over her, making her hug the dressing gown even tighter around her, 'so I'll bid you goodnight.'

She stood watching as he returned

to his car and then closed the door. She went back upstairs, inexplicably comforted by the knowledge that he cared enough about her to call and check when he suspected something might be wrong. She dismissed the notion that it was a bit of a coincidence him turning up on her doorstep right after she'd found her kitchen lights blazing and the window wide open to the elements. Perhaps she ought to get some bolts fitted to the front door. That way, even with a key, no-one could enter.

Why on earth hadn't she thought of that before?

* ★ *

Saturday morning duly came round and Jazz wasted no time setting out for the manor house. There was still a great deal to do. She took her dress with her, plus an overnight bag. She'd barely seen Zak since he'd called to check she was okay, and, in his absence, had somehow managed to wipe all memories of him and Sara together from her mind. If only she could erase the memories of the frightening events of the past weeks with equal success.

Thelma greeted her warmly. 'I've made up a bedroom for you. I'll take you up and you can leave your things there.' Her eagle-eyed gaze took in the dress in its large protective bag; Jazz hadn't wanted to put it into the small case for fear of irredeemably creasing it. 'Is that the dress?'

Jazz nodded.

'Can I have a look when we get to your room?' She sounded as excited as if it were her that was going to be wearing it.

'Of course you can and you can tell me what you think of it.'

Once they had reached the bedroom, she unpacked the dress and held it up against her.

Thelma gasped. 'Oh, it's beautiful and so-o your colour.'

'Do you think so?'

'I do. You'll be the belle of the evening, I'm sure. Now,' she indicated the bedroom, 'is this okay for you?'

For the first time Jazz looked around her. Wow! Is it okay? What a silly question. The room dwarfed her bedroom at Cliff House and was considerably more luxuriously appointed. Wardrobes lined the whole of one wall, with a huge vanity unit and illuminated mirror on another. Floor to ceiling windows stretched all the way along a third. There was a four poster bed and Thelma led her into a bathroom that contained every luxury she'd ever dreamed of.

'It's perfect, Thelma; thank you.'

'Well now, you unpack and while you're doing that I'll brew us a pot of coffee and then we can get started.'

Once they'd drunk every drop of coffee and consumed a couple of croissants each, they began their preparations for the evening. While Thelma made a start on the food, Jazz saw to the dining room, laying the table with exquisite Irish linen placemats and napkins, silver cutlery, and ending with some extremely fine crystal glasses — Waterford, she guessed — three at each place setting, for red and white wine and water. Finally, she laid out the place cards according to the seating plan which she and Zak had worked on together. She'd just finished that when the doorbell chimed.

'I'll get it — ' she sang out to Thelma. It was the flower arrangements that she'd ordered. She'd specified two large ones for the dining table, so she set those down immediately, placing tall candlesticks between them and on either side. The remainder she spread around the house in the positions she'd already decided on. The perfume of the white lilies and roses was heady and seductive and would greet the guests as they walked into the hallway.

By late afternoon, all that could be done was done and they could relax over a cup of tea. They'd just settled themselves in Thelma's small sitting room off the kitchen when they heard the front door opening. In the next second, Zak was striding into the kitchen, calling, 'Thelma, I'm back — '

Thelma was instantly on her feet, almost running to meet him. 'I'm here.'

'Has Jazz arrived?'

'Yes, she's in my sitting room.'

Jazz also got to her feet, but more slowly than Thelma, and she walked into the kitchen. Zak's gaze flew to her, and sharpened as he took in the sight of her. 'You look worn out — ' he bluntly said, his gaze raking her from head to toe.

'Gee, thanks for that,' she instantly bit back.

'Sorry; that sounded rude.'

Jazz didn't respond.

'Been enjoying some more late night viewing?' He was referring to the other evening when he'd called in. Jazz again didn't reply. 'The house looks superb,' he went on, obviously trying to placate her in the wake of his tactless remark. 'And smells equally superb,' he added with a wry smile.

Oh Lord, she'd overdone it.

'Still, I'm sure the ladies will appreciate it. Not sure about the men, though.' Then he was grinning broadly and she realised he was teasing her. She couldn't prevent her own grin in response, even though she'd resolved to keep her distance, not to allow herself to grow any closer to him than she already had. After all, by the look and sound of things, he was back with Sara.

'If you'll excuse me,' she said, 'I think I'll go to my room and prepare myself for the evening. Um — are there any extra guests to be accommodated?' Belatedly, she wondered whether Sara would be coming this evening.

Zak looked at her, his brow dragged down in a frown. 'No, should there be?'

'Oh no,' Jazz breezily assured him, trying to ignore the lifting of her spirit and the increased beat of her heart. Could Beth have possibly got it all wrong — or rather, had Sara's mother? Maybe Zak and Sara weren't an item, after all? If they were, then surely Sara would be coming this evening — unless Zak was loath to depose Jazz from the role of hostess after all her efforts; afraid of hurting her feelings? Yes, that must be it — although he hadn't seemed bothered about hurting her feelings just minutes ago.

'Okay, off you go then.' He'd been holding a stack of envelopes when he'd come in — the day's postal delivery, she presumed — and he started to sort through it now. He stopped abruptly upon seeing one particular envelope. It was mauve-tinted. The sort of envelope a woman would use. Jazz watched as his expression changed — clearly he recognised the hand writing on the front — and he swung to leave the room, presumably to open and read it in private.

It must be from Sara. And if it was, it must mean they were back together.

14

The first of the guests to arrive that evening was an overweight, rather plain woman and her considerably more attractive husband. Zak introduced them to Jazz as Sam and Diana Forsyth. They were both in their early forties, Jazz estimated, and, in her opinion, couldn't look more ill-suited. This was born out by the way Sam's eyes lit up when they rested upon Jazz.

'Jazz?' was his initial exclamation. 'That's an unusual name — '

'It's short for Jasmine,' Jazz told him. 'My mother had an exotic taste in names.'

Sam's eyes, she noted, roamed boldly over her. Zak's gaze had followed the same route but, with him, it had felt different. Zak's expression had been warm with admiration as he'd murmured, 'Good choice of dress. It's definitely your colour.'

This man's eyes contained a lustful quality and his gaze lingered a bit too long on Jazz's cleavage. His wife noticed, as did Zak. A look of bitter resignation came over Diana's face; whereas Zak's expression darkened, almost threateningly. Luckily, four more people arrived and the moment passed. For an instant, though, Jazz had glimpsed anger within Zak, which led her to think he was far from indifferent to her — whatever his feelings for the absent Sara. However, if he was getting back with Sara, then he shouldn't be revealing any emotions at all towards her. It suggested a very fickle nature. Something she hadn't expected of him.

It was eight thirty by the time the last of the guests had arrived. More than one of the men exhibited a high degree of interest in her. An elderly man even went so far as to slyly ask, 'So, are you Zak's latest girlfriend?'

'No,' Jazz replied, 'I'm his PA.'

'Same thing, isn't it?' he laughed,

winking at her and making Jazz wonder what he got up to at work with his own PA.

'Not at all,' she firmly replied. 'Zak and I have a purely professional relationship.'

'Is that really what you believe?' He slipped an arm around her waist and brought his head close to hers. 'So — how do you explain the fact that Zak's eyes are boring into me so hard, I can practically feel the darned things drilling holes into my flesh?'

Jazz was stunned. Even so, she couldn't resist slanting a glance across the room at Zak, only to find him indeed staring at her and the older man, his look one of brooding as heavy lids hooded his eyes, and his mouth clamped itself into a grim line.

'See,' the old man murmured. 'If you believe he regards you as merely his PA then you aren't as bright as you seem.' And with a chuckle, he strolled away to join his silver-haired wife and another couple.

Thelma chose that moment to appear and announce that dinner was served. Jazz didn't know whether to be relieved or disappointed. The expression that had been in Zak's eyes just then gave her plenty of ammunition for thought. It hadn't been the expression of a man involved romantically with another woman.

Dinner passed off successfully, with Thelma receiving many compliments on the food as she served it. Jazz also was on the receiving end of much praise for her management of the evening. Sam kept looking her way, she noticed. It earned Jazz a series of glares from his wife. The man at her side also displayed a warm interest in her, managing to touch her often enough to force Jazz to move her chair slightly to one side, away from him.

As for Zak, he only glanced briefly at her now and then from where he sat at the opposite end of the table to her. He was very much involved with the attractive woman on his right. She kept up a flirtatious dialogue with him, making him laugh out loud several times. What was strange was that the man with whom the woman had arrived showed no displeasure at this. As their surnames were different, Jazz could only assume they weren't married, and maybe weren't even a couple — not in the accepted sense of the word, at any rate. Jazz did hear her ask at one point how Sara was. But, despite Jazz leaning perilously far across the table, on the pretext of straightening a rose that had begun to wilt from the heat of a candle flame, she couldn't make out what Zak answered.

By the time everyone had drunk their coffee and begun to drift away, Jazz felt exhausted. She'd curtailed her wine consumption and stuck mainly to water, not wanting to lose control of herself as she'd done at the hotel. She hadn't noticed how much Zak had drunk.

The last guest didn't depart until past one o'clock and Jazz's eyes were literally aching with the need for sleep. Thelma had long since retired, so Zak and Jazz were left entirely alone.

'That went well,' he said as he headed for the kitchen, several empty wine glasses balanced precariously in each hand. Jazz winced to hear them jangling against each other, fully expecting to see them break, or at the very least, crack. 'Thanks to your expert organisation.' He paused and then went on, 'Sam seemed to take to you. He couldn't take his eyes off you, in fact. Mind you, not many of the men could. The one at your side seemed unable to keep his hands to himself, either.'

So, he had noticed what had been happening then, despite his apparent fascination with the woman at his side? A surge of indignation arose within Jazz. His tone suggested that he was blaming her for her dinner companion's touchy-feely behaviour. And who was he to disapprove of anything anyone else did, when he was apparently in a relationship with one woman while displaying possessive jealousy over another? Or was she reading it all wrong and he was simply disgusted with her?

She couldn't help it; she instantly retaliated. 'Oh, and there I was thinking that you were totally absorbed in Miss Congeniality at your side.'

He swivelled his head to look directly at her then. 'My, my, where did that come from?' he murmured. 'You sound almost — well, jealous.'

She couldn't believe what she was hearing. 'Jealous? Why on earth should I be jealous? It's your house, your dinner party; it's entirely up to you how you behave.'

Zak didn't at first respond to that. He strode into the kitchen and placed the glasses he'd been holding onto the worktop. Then, he swung to face her. Jazz was quite close to him, she'd also been carrying glasses. She too put them down, rather more carefully than Zak had. Their hands were almost touching at that point, so it didn't take much for him to lift his arms and grip her by the shoulders, roughly swinging her to face him, as he muttered, 'Yes, it is, isn't it? So — here goes — ' and he dragged her towards him, ignoring her gasp of shock as their chests collided, and he brought his head down and clamped his lips over hers.

Jazz couldn't move. The last thing she'd expected to happen was this. She'd anticipated an analysis of the evening: the food; a discussion of the guests and their behaviour; their conversations even — what she hadn't expected was to be kissed. And it wasn't any ordinary kiss. It was one that was filled with hunger, his lips urgently moving on hers, bruising, hard — She couldn't help but respond, even when his hands began tracing her curves, gently cupping them, pulling her so close she could feel his arousal. She parted her lips for him, helpless beneath the strength of her desire. Her heart throbbed, the blood coursing hotly through her. His mouth left hers and travelled down the arch of her throat, before moving on to where her dress dipped between her breasts. It wasn't until he groaned her name that she came to her senses.

What were they doing? What was he doing? He was, from what she'd heard and witnessed, involved with another woman. So why was he now kissing her? Did he think she was that — easily available; that cheap?

She shoved him away from her, so hard he staggered backwards. 'What the hell do you think you're doing?'

He gave a throaty laugh. 'Do I really need to explain? You can't be that innocent.' He made to pull her back into his arms. She gave another push.

'I mean it — stop it.'

He literally froze. His mouth twisted, a white line encircling it. 'What's wrong? We both want this — '

'No, I don't. How dare you?'

He snorted, his gaze narrowing at her. 'Well, you could have fooled me.

One minute you were all pliant and eager, very eager. The next you're acting all coy and missish. It doesn't suit you.'

'How dare you?'

'Yes, yes, you've already asked me that once,' he retorted. The anger seemed to have evaporated as he spoke. All she could glimpse now upon his face was weary resignation. 'Oh, this is too stupid to be true. We're both adults — ' He stared at her, his eyes bleak and weary. 'Just go to bed, Jazz.'

His top lip curled at her, his contempt only too visible. Jazz felt real fury then. He was looking at her with contempt — after the way in which he'd just behaved? Like a two-timing, double-crossing — didn't he care about Sara? About hurting her — Jazz?

'We've said enough — done enough for now. I'll see you in the morning.'

Oh no you won't, was all Jazz could think. She wasn't staying here for another second, never mind all night. In fact, she wouldn't ever enter this house

276

again. He'd just confirmed her opinion of the majority of men. You couldn't trust any of them. Her car was outside. She'd had very little to drink. She'd drive home.

She swung and swept up the stairs to her room; she could feel his eyes boring into her as she went. It was a matter of minutes to change her clothes back into what she'd worn to come here in the first place, and then pack the few things she'd brought with her. The dress she left lying, neatly folded, on the bed. She didn't want it. Let him give it to Sara. She wanted nothing to remind her of — of him, or tonight. The only thing left to do was to write a letter of resignation from her job. She did, at least, owe him that much.

Luckily, she'd noticed a notepad in one of the drawers in the vanity unit earlier. She took it out now and scrawled a few words across a single sheet informing him of her intention, before placing it on top of the discarded

dress where either he or Thelma
— Thelma probably — couldn't fail to
see it. Then, very quietly, she left the
room and descended the stairs to go
out through the front door.

15

The drive home was a treacherous one for Jazz. Not only were the roads icy, there was also a freezing fog. It obscured anything further than a couple of metres ahead. She inched along, scared to move at more than a crawl and, all the time, bitterly regretting her decision to drive in such dangerous conditions. This was all down to Zak Rivers. If he hadn't tried to make love to her, she wouldn't have rushed out of his house and she wouldn't be in such a dire predicament now. If she crashed, it would be his fault.

Eventually, she reached Cliff House, where, shivering with a combination of coldness and exhaustion, she thankfully made her way to the kitchen and the heat of the Aga. She made herself a hot drink and, huddled in a chair, sipped at it as she once more went over the events of the evening. Why had he kissed her if his relationship with Sara was back on? Had he even considered if such behaviour was fair to either one of them? If she hadn't told Beth she would say nothing, she would have come right out with it and asked him.

Worn out and deeply unhappy, she eventually dragged herself to bed, only to lie, replaying the scene between her and Zak over and over in her head. She did finally fall into exhausted slumber to be woken only minutes later it seemed by the sound of the phone ringing on her bedside table. Half asleep still, she lifted the receiver to her ear.

'What the hell does this note mean?' a deep voice growled.

It was Zak and he sounded furious. Thelma evidently hadn't wasted any time giving him her note.

Jazz sat bolt upright, struggling to banish the lingering dregs of sleep. She'd need a clear head to deal with

Zak in this mood. She glanced at the clock on her bedside table. It was only seven thirty, for goodness sake. She hadn't got to bed until gone three. And how had Thelma known she'd left, anyway? Of course — she'd left the bedroom door open. She should have closed it behind her; she wouldn't have been woken up at this ungodly hour then. 'I would have thought it self-explanatory. I've resigned.'

'You can't resign — over a bit of lovemaking, for God's sake, and I presume that's what all this is about? This isn't the nineteenth century; it's the twenty first.'

'Maybe it is, but I can't go on working for a man who behaves in such a manner.'

'I don't believe I'm hearing this — ' She heard his snort of incredulity as clearly as if he were in the room with her, 'a man who behaves in such a manner?' He skilfully mimicked her tone and words. 'You sound like some damned Victorian heroine — all outrage because a man demonstrates a perfectly natural desire for her. What's wrong with that? Or haven't you ever been kissed before?'

She gave what she hoped was a cool laugh but suspected it was, in reality, a slightly hysterical one, 'Of course I have.'

'Then what's the big deal?'

'The big deal is — ' she angrily began, intending to ask him exactly what he thought he was doing, stringing two women along in such a callous fashion, or at least trying to — when she remembered her promise to Beth and abruptly stopped speaking.

'Well, do go on. This I can't wait to hear. What precisely is the big deal?' His voice was ragged; harsh.

'I don't get romantically involved with my employers. I never have and I never will. Business and- and — '

'And-and what?' He was mimicking her again, sarcastically and cruelly.

Somehow — she didn't quite know how — she managed to stay calm. 'I've always found that business and-and pleasure don't mix.' She knew she sounded exactly like the prim Victorian heroine he'd accused her of being, but she couldn't help herself. And what else could she say if she couldn't accuse him of trying to have an affair with two women at the same time?

'I presume you mean sex; business and sex don't mix? Lord — give me strength,' he muttered. 'Okay, how about this then — Don't go on working for me. I can easily find someone else to act as my PA. Come out with me this evening instead.'

'No, sorry, that won't be possible,' and she firmly replaced the receiver, afraid that the small sob lurking at the back of her throat would finally break free. And the last thing she wanted was for Zak to hear her weeping over him and his uncaring attitude to both her and Sara. Which meant that — even if he ended it with Sara — how could she, Jazz, possibly trust him — ever again? If he'd treat one woman like that, he'd have no compunction in treating another — her, in fact — with the same cruel disregard.

As early as it was and as tired as she was, she knew that after their row returning to sleep would be impossible. Instead, she got up, to stand at the window, gazing out onto the frosty, sunlit morning. The fog had completely vanished, leaving in its wake a clear sky. She'd have a walk, she decided. Maybe, just maybe, physical exercise would dislodge and hopefully banish all thoughts of Zak and the kisses that they had exchanged the night before, extinguish the feel of his arms about her, of his lips moving on hers, of her own passionate response and the fact that he must now be aware of how she felt about him.

She sighed. She wouldn't go into town though; she couldn't face meeting anyone that she knew, especially not Beth. She'd be bound to ask how the dinner party had gone and that was something Jazz really didn't want to discuss. But apart from that natural reluctance, conversation and local gossip were the last things she needed; she also suspected that Beth would swiftly detect her misery and want to know what had caused it. The older woman could, at times, be surprisingly intuitive.

So, instead, she turned and headed in the opposite direction, walking along the cliff top for a short way and then following the road down into Porth Brennan, where she sat, huddled in her coat, on the deserted beach, gazing out over the sea towards the distant horizon. She was hoping that the early morning peace, the solitude, would offer her some comfort, ease her aching heart. It didn't. The mournful calls of the gulls wheeling overhead simply deepened her unhappiness.

What was she going to do? It was a question she was asking more and more frequently. Stay here in St. Kernan or sell up and return to Worcestershire? One thing she would do — one mystery she could clear up was the reason for Emily and Serena's life changing row. She picked up the phone the second she got inside the house and dialled her parents' Spanish number.

It was Serena who answered. 'Hello?'

'Mum, it's me — '

'Jazz, is everything all right?'

'Mum, I have to ask — ' It was imperative all of a sudden that she know the truth of what had happened between the two sisters.

'Yes?'

'What happened between you and Aunt Emily? What was so serious that it stopped me from visiting her?'

'Aah. I've been expecting you to ask for some time now.'

'So — tell me.'

'Promise you'll never bring it up in front of your father.'

Jazz hesitated, thinking of what she'd agreed to with Beth and its unforeseen consequences. 'We-ell, it depends on what you tell me.'

'No, you must promise or I won't tell

you. It's all way in the past — I don't want it dragged up again, especially not now, in the wake of Emily's death.'

Jazz had no choice, not if she wanted to know the truth. 'Okay, okay, I promise.'

Her mother sighed with relief. 'I had reason to suspect that — that — '

'Yes, yes,' Jazz urged.

'That your father and Emily were having — ' There was another pause, a longer one this time. Jazz wanted to scream at her mother 'Get on with it'. She didn't, of course. Mainly because she had an awful premonition of what it was Serena was about to tell her, ' — having an affair.'

Even though she'd guessed what was coming, to hear it actually said out loud was almost more than Jazz could bear. 'Hang on, you only suspected?'

'Yes.'

'Didn't you ask them?'

'Of course I did. They denied it, naturally. Emily was furious with me and refused to speak to me again.'

'But — you stopped me from going there.'

'I know, Jazz, and I bitterly regret that now. But it was always your father that fetched you and I didn't — well, I didn't want to put temptation in his way. If it hadn't actually happened, it most certainly might have. Your father made no secret of his admiration for Emily. She was always so much cleverer, smarter than me. I was sure that one day he'd — '

'Did you ever find out if it was true or not?'

'Yes.'

'And was it?'

'It wasn't. I jumped to conclusions, the wrong conclusions — I'm sorry.'

Jazz was too angry to speak for a moment. 'So — why didn't you let me come here again when you knew the truth?'

'I don't know. As I said, I was always afraid — there was an attraction between them, Jazz; it was all too obvious — to me, at any rate. I sometimes think that was why Emily never married — no other man came up to your father. Emily never forgave me for suspecting her of such a betrayal or for stopping you from visiting her, so we never spoke again.'

* * *

That night it was the noise of something banging downstairs that woke her. She sat up. This couldn't be happening? She'd had security bolts fitted to the front and back doors; no-one could possibly get in — not even if they were in possession of a key.

She listened again. It sounded like a window. Could she have left one open? Surely not; she was always so careful, meticulously checking everything before she came up to bed. In fact, she was becoming borderline OCD about it all.

She gave a weary sigh. She'd have to go and check, she'd get no rest otherwise — not that she expected to find anything — or anyone. As she always did, she grabbed hold of the cricket bat — just in case this time was different.

The banging grew louder as she descended the stairs. It was coming from the kitchen. At least there were no lights on this time. She peered in around the open door, and just as she'd thought, a window was open — hang on; she stared, incredulously. They were all open; the two side ones and the transom.

She knew she hadn't opened them. She ran to close them. It had been raining and the sill inside had puddles of water along it. She grabbed a tea towel and mopped it up, asking herself how someone could have done this? There was no sign of the windows having been forced. They'd been opened from the inside — so whoever had done that had already been in the house.

Oh no! The house couldn't really be haunted, could it? She couldn't believe it; refused to believe it. A small sound to one side of her had her turning her head. A saucepan sat on the Aga and it was steaming; something was bubbling inside. Frightened by this time at what she might find, she reached out and lifted the pan off the hob. Gingerly, she lifted the lid and looked inside. It was full of boiling water; nothing else, just water.

With shaking hands she poured it down the sink, her thoughts in turmoil. She hadn't put the pan there — so who had? It took a couple more moments before she became aware of other sounds; foot-steps. Someone was upstairs.

She slammed the pan down onto the draining board. She'd had enough of this. Sheer anger propelled her across the kitchen and up the stairs; effectively obliterating any fear of what she might find when she got to the top. She was going to sort this out — for once and for all. She reached the landing and sped towards the guest room. She flung the door open to discover, as usual, an empty room.

Panting, she dropped down onto the bed. She must be hearing things? It was the only explanation. Could it be some sort of mental breakdown? Could she, in fact, be doing it all herself — while sleep walking maybe? No, she'd never walked in her sleep, not even as a child, and anyway, it wouldn't explain the footsteps, the piano playing or the whispering. She definitely hadn't done any of those things.

She returned to the kitchen and slammed the windows shut, then went up to her bedroom. She'd go and see a doctor tomorrow and get some sleeping tablets. Or maybe tranquillisers would be more appropriate?

Worn out and full of a bottomless despair, she fell asleep — and again Emily appeared to her, her eyes dark and haunted, her arms outstretched.

Jazz woke. 'Emily,' she cried, pushing herself up in bed, 'what is it? Tell me — please — help me!'

But, of course, she wasn't there.

* * *

The following morning, she went to see the local doctor but, as she was reluctant to tell him exactly what was happening to her, for fear he'd have her committed as mentally insane, he refused to prescribe either sleeping tablets or tranquillisers.

'If something's bothering you,' he said, 'I can refer you for counselling — It's much the better way.'

She declined and returned home.

That night, it was the whispering that she heard. She lay, for several moments, struggling to distinguish the words, before thinking — she couldn't go on like this. She had to find out the truth — once and for all — and she wouldn't stop till she had. She'd done it with her mother, she could do it with this, and if she was going mad, well — she'd deal with that too. Either way, she was going to uncover the truth of what was happening here, in this house.

Without making a sound, she started

down the stairs, every two or three steps stopping to listen, trying to pinpoint where the voice was coming from. It was definitely coming from the hallway. She reached the bottom of the stairs and stood motionless, head tilted, listening. She realised then the voice was coming from high up, from the top of the cloaks cupboard, in fact.

She inched slowly towards it. It was definitely a voice but the words were still unintelligible, just a low, murmuring sound. Carefully, soundlessly, she lifted the chair that stood to one side and, placing it in front of the cupboard, clambered up onto it. And there it was, a small loudspeaker right at the back, where she would never have spotted it if she hadn't got up and looked; and the voice was coming out of it.

Finally, an explanation, and it wasn't a supernatural one. She also wasn't losing her mind. Her relief was short-lived, though, because someone had done this; someone intent on terrifying her.

She studied the speaker intently. A wire ran inconspicuously up the wall and through a hole drilled into the ceiling. She wouldn't notice it unless she knew it was there. It would lead directly into the guest bedroom next to hers, where presumably shc would find another concealed loudspeaker. A wire also disappeared down into the back of the cupboard. She scrambled off the chair and knelt down. It exited out at the bottom again, from where it ran around the base of the skirting of the hall and into the dining room — again, relatively inconspicuously. Nevertheless, it explained everything: the footsteps she'd heard, the whispering voice, the piano playing — it was all piped via the speakers throughout the house. Everything that she'd heard had been a recording. It had to be. There was no other explanation. All she had to do was find the recorder.

But someone had to enter the house to turn it on, and with the bolts on the doors — she frowned. It also failed to explain the open windows, the writing on the glass, the pan of water, the lights and the radio left on. Whoever it was had access to the house, and as she'd already reasoned, it couldn't be with a key. So how was it being done?

She went into the dining room and found the wire there; in a tiny gap between the panelled walls and the floor. She began to inspect the panelling. There had to be a speaker somewhere, somehow — because the music had always seemed to come from this room. She realised that the whispering had stopped. Whoever was doing this must have heard her moving around.

Using her fingertips now, she felt slowly across the wood, tapping, searching for something — anything. After several minutes, she heard the click that she'd heard twice before as a panel swung inwards, right in front of her. It was a door, skilfully concealed, but, nonetheless, a door. She leapt backwards, crying out in her shock.

Once her initial panic faded, she leant forwards and looked through the gap. The first thing she saw was a steep flight of stone steps leading straight down — into total darkness. She ran back into the hallway and fetched a torch that she kept in the cupboard. She then returned to the doorway and shone the beam of light down.

With her heart in her mouth, she descended the steps to find herself in an underground chamber. It must lie beneath the dining room and part of the lounge. So Zak had been right about the cellar. How had he known? Had he made a search while the house was empty, because Emily couldn't have told him about it? Jazz was sure she hadn't known. She'd have told her niece. He could have used the key concealed beneath the stone and found this room — before she'd even moved in. He'd have had plenty of time to install the speakers throughout the house.

She shone the beam of the torch

around, no-one was there, whoever had been down here had gone; she did, however, discover the evidence that she sought.

On a small wooden box, pushed back against a wall, was a small cassette player — and there were the cassettes by the side of it. Wires led from the player, both up the wall into the dining room, from where it would run on to the various speakers and a power supply, as well as down to an extension box on the floor of the chamber. There were several partly burned down candles placed on a narrow ledge on one wall, presumably for light.

She climbed back up the stairs and found the socket and plug beneath the sideboard in the dining room. There was also a tiny speaker.

She returned to the chamber and pressed the play button on the recorder. Instantly, the whispering began. She swapped the cassette for another, and this time piano music poured out. The last one held the sound of footsteps.

She switched it off. There was just one question remaining. How had the culprit got down here, if there was no access to the house by conventional means?

Shining the beam of the torch about her once more, she saw what looked like some sort of entrance. She crossed to it and saw a narrow tunnel sloping steeply downwards. Whoever had been here moments ago, operating the recorder, must have escaped along it when they heard the sounds of her moving, searching — in the dining room.

Grasping the torch even more tightly, she started to walk down it. With every step that she took, her certainty grew that it would lead her to the beach below Cliff House. The ground beneath her feet was uneven and slippery. She'd have to be careful. The last thing she needed was to fall and injure herself. No one knew where she was.

Alarm knifed through her at the thought, and also at the notion that the intruder had had unhindered access to her home. He could have got in whenever she was out, connected and disconnected any of the speakers he wanted, making it seem that the piano music came only from the dining room, the whispering from the hallway, the footsteps from the bedroom — He could even have attacked her in her bed had he so chosen.

Quickening her pace, she carried on down the tunnel. There was a dank, musty odour. She wrinkled her nose. It was coming from the walls, they were running with damp. She swung the torch beam around and spotted something lying on the ground a couple of feet ahead. What was it? Jazz reached it. It was a scarf.

With a stabbing of dismay, Jazz recognised it. It was Joel's. The scarf his mother had given him. He must have dropped it in his rush to escape. She picked it up. It was very silky, which would explain why it had slid off unnoticed — he never tied it.

She leant against the wall, oblivious now to the damp seeping into her sleeve, shock making her tremble. Joel was the last person she'd suspected. He'd been her friend.

Tears stung her eyes as she turned around to return the way she'd come. She didn't need to go on. She could hear the sea crashing onto the shore below. Joel's house lay on the opposite side of the cove to Cliff House. He must have found the entrance to the tunnel at some time — it was probably in one of the many caves that dotted the base of the cliffs hereabouts — decided to explore it and somehow discovered the entrance into Cliff House. It was very convenient. He'd only have to walk a little way along the beach to gain access and, in the dead of night, no-one would see him — although, the entrance to the tunnel couldn't be that obvious or surely it would be generally known about? Emily would have known — wouldn't she? And she couldn't have. She'd have had the entrance into the dining room sealed up at the very least.

The important question was — how long had Joel known about it? And had he been doing the same thing to Emily?

Jazz pulled herself together and, oblivious now to the risk of slipping, ran back to the house. Once she was in the dining room, she closed the panelling door and dragged the heavy table over, tipping it onto its side to stand in front of the opening. Not that it would stop anyone who was determined enough from entering but it made her feel slightly safer. First thing tomorrow, she'd get rid of all the things in the chamber and then have the door permanently sealed.

She spent the remainder of the night sitting in the kitchen, drinking cup after cup of strong tea, waiting for dawn to break. She intended to confront Joel with what she'd discovered. She wasn't afraid. She didn't think he'd hurt her; he could have done that at any time. No, he just wanted to scare her into selling Cliff House to him and Blake. Just for once, he wanted to best Zak.

By the time dawn broke, she was dressed ready for her walk along the lane, and she left the house, grimly determined to have this out with him.

16

It was a matter of minutes for Jazz to reach Joel's house, where Joel immediately opened the door at her knock, despite the early hour. His gaze dropped to the scarf she was holding. He didn't look surprised, so she assumed he'd guessed already that she'd discovered what he'd been doing. He'd probably heard her in the dining room and made his escape before she could find him down there — in person. He'd probably hoped she'd think it was Zak behind it all — until he realised he'd dropped his scarf.

'Jazz,' he began haltingly, 'I'm sorry — '

'I bet you are, sorry you've been found out,' she cried, furiously brandishing the scarf at him as she followed him inside. 'How could you? How could you scare me like that? All alone as I was. Were you doing the same thing to Emily?'

'No. I wouldn't have done that. She was a lovely lady, and it was her home.' He looked genuinely shocked that she could think that. Jazz felt a surge of relief. 'I-I don't know what got into me. But — I'd heard you were planning on living in the house and once I'd had the idea and realised the potential of it to make you sell and leave — well, I couldn't resist it. I'm so sorry, but I've been desperate, otherwise I would never have — and it hadn't ever been your home, not really.'

Jazz interrupted impatiently. She was having a struggle to hide her fury with him; her contempt. 'But it's my home now, Joel.' She took a deep breath. She needed to know everything. 'Was it just you, or is Blake Carlisle involved too?'

'No! God, no! I was doing it alone. You see — we need to expand. He's been talking about closing down a couple of sites and writing off the losses. They're the ones I manage, actually, as well as part own. I can't afford to invest any more money to save them, so I stand to lose everything; my job, even. I'd be virtually bankrupt. But I shouldn't have done it, I know that. There's no excuse — other than the need to supply Blake with another site to develop, here in St. Kernan, to make a profit on; to subsidise the ones that we're making losses on. A luxury site would have done that. If you'd just agreed to sell to us, all this would have been avoided — ' he burst out.

Jazz regarded him in astonishment. 'Are you trying to make this my fault?'

'No.'

She eyed him then, her curiosity getting the better of her. 'When did you do all the wiring? I mean — that must have taken a considerable time.'

'A short while before you moved in. It didn't take that long — an afternoon. It was easy once I'd worked out how to do it, it seemed worth a try.'

It seemed worth a try? She was aware of a feeling of utter repugnance for Joel and the fact that he had embarked, so casually, upon a campaign of terror — because that's what it had been — without a thought for her state of mind. In that moment, it was all she could do to go on talking to him. 'How did you find the tunnel and the concealed door?'

'I discovered the entrance to the tunnel when I was a boy. I'd been exploring one particular cave when I noticed a strange looking rock just propped up for no apparent reason. It must have been there for a very long time, it was covered in lichen and all sorts. Anyway, I managed to squeeze behind it and I found the tunnel. It must have originally been used for smuggling, I think, and someone had concealed it. I followed it along and found the chamber and the door into the dining room. It's far more obvious from the tunnel side than it is from inside. Out of curiosity, I opened it. I didn't go in — not then. I was going to tell you all about it but you didn't come here again. So, I more or less forgot about it and then, when I heard that you'd definitely refused to sell — well, I remembered it and had the idea of the tape recording. I'd seen an old film in which someone did a similar thing. I'm so sorry. I don't know what possessed me. My only excuse is I was desperate.' He eyed her. 'Are you going to tell the police?'

For the first time then, he looked genuinely frightened. Jazz was sorely tempted to say yes; she ought to say yes. But, 'No, on the condition that you remove every last wire, the loudspeakers, the recorder, everything — and you are never to come to Cliff House ever again. I'll get the door into the dining room secured, and have the tunnel entrance into the chamber blocked as well.'

He nodded, looking close to tears. Jazz felt an unexpected pang of sympathy for him then. 'I'll take everything away and then I'll personally do all that you've just mentioned. It's the least I can do.'

'Thank you,' and without another word she left.

*　*　*

It was later that morning that Jazz's doorbell rang. Thinking it would be Joel come to undo his handiwork, she yanked the door open and said, 'Joel — come — oh, it's you.'

It was Zak. 'Sorry to disappoint you,' he bit out.

Jazz didn't respond. She simply stood and waited for him to say whatever he'd come to say.

'Aren't you going to ask me in then?'

Jazz shrugged and turned to lead the way into the sitting room. Once there, she swung back to him and asked, 'So — what is it? I'm not coming back to work for you if that's why you're here.'

'Not even if I promise not to kiss you again?' There was a determined look to him, as well as a very disturbing gleam in his eye. He was also standing way too

309

close. She inched away.

'Not even then. Why don't you ask Sara instead?'

Zak frowned. 'Why on earth should I ask Sara?'

'Well, you're seeing her, aren't you?'

He was beginning to look bemused. 'I have seen her — yes.'

Was there no shame in the man? Chasing around after her, when — 'I saw you,' she burst out, 'holding hands, you kissing hers, in a cafe in Truro.'

'Aah — ' His eyes narrowed then at her.

'So how could you have the-the barefaced cheek to make love to me?'

'Yeah, how could I?' He cocked his head to one side as he asked, 'But tell me, Jazz, didn't you enjoy it — just a little? I certainly did. And so, I suspect — if we're being absolutely honest here, did you. If not, then you're a fantastic actress. So good, in fact, you should be on the stage.'

Jazz was mesmerised now by the expression on his face. He looked

— well, almost triumphant.

'Look, Jazz, I'm not a fool. If you didn't care for me, you wouldn't be so bothered about a kiss.'

'It's-it's shameless, contemptible — to kiss me when you're with someone else.'

'But, you see, I'm not with someone else.'

'You-you're not?'

'No. What you saw was me comforting Sara because she'd just been dumped by the man that she truly loves. She and I did enjoy a brief flirtation a while ago, but that's all it was. I was merely offering her some advice on winning him back and it's paid off I'm pleased to say, because I've received an invitation to their wedding.'

'Was that the tinted envelope?'

He nodded. 'So, when I kissed you, I wasn't involved with anyone else other than you. And I was very involved with you as I recall. So — does that go some way to explaining things?'

He had inched closer to her again.

When had he done that? She hadn't noticed. She took a couple of steps back. He made no move to close the gap between them.

'So — why didn't you kiss me at the hotel? I mean — I practically threw myself at you.'

'I'm not in the habit of taking advantage of a woman who'd had more to drink than she was accustomed to. As I believe I said then, I like my woman to be fully aware of what she's doing and what she wants.' His gaze smouldered at her.

His woman — she was his woman. A hot flame tore through her.

'Jazz, I've fallen in love with you.' He moved closer again until she could feel his warm breath feathering her skin. This time she didn't move away. Instead, she closed her eyes in anticipation of his kiss, only to open them again when it didn't come. 'I kissed you the night of the dinner party because, frankly, I couldn't help myself. I'd had to watch men flirting with you all evening and, frankly, enough was enough. I fell for you the first second practically that I saw you — on the cliff top — out there.' He indicated the back garden. 'Remember?'

'Oh yes.' As if she could ever forget.

'So — I wasn't being unfaithful to Sara. I was being faithful to my own heart and desires.' His voice was raw with passion.

Jazz heard it and couldn't speak. Yet, there was one more thing she needed to know. 'My aunt Emily — did you put pressure on her to sell Cliff House, because you were seen coming here and her lease on the shop — which you own — was due for renewal?'

'Did Scott tell you that?'

She nodded. She wouldn't tell him what else Joel had been up to, at least not now. Who knew how he'd react, so deep was his dislike of the other man?

'Just a minute — ' it was now his turn to take a couple of steps backwards, 'are you asking if I was blackmailing your aunt? No sale, no lease?' He looked genuinely shocked. 'Is that what he told you?'

Her heart sank. Had she, with those few words, ruined everything? 'Well, not precisely — no. Not in those exact words.'

'I did make her an offer on Cliff House — as I did to you — just to see if she would be interested in selling — I'd long had my eyes on it for a luxury hotel — but when she refused that was it, I accepted that. As to the shop, yes, her lease was due for renewal and that's why I visited her. She wanted to buy the freehold. It didn't happen because, sadly, she died first. I had a great respect for Emily. I would never have done anything to hurt or distress her. And just for the record, I've long since abandoned my plans for Cliff House. It's you I want, nothing else — '

Jazz didn't try to hide her relief. She hadn't spoilt things. She beamed ecstatically at him.

He grinned and held out his arms. 'So — with that all cleared up, can I kiss you — without you spitting at me like a wild cat and demanding to know, in that icy tone of yours, precisely what I'm doing?'

'Oh, Zak,' and she did as he so clearly wanted and moved into his arms.

Zak didn't hesitate. He bent his head and captured her lips. 'Oh, Jazz,' he murmured, 'I love you so much. Say you'll marry me — '

This time it was Jazz who didn't hesitate. 'I will, because, you see, I love you too — '

THE END

We do hope that you have enjoyed reading this large print book.

Did you know that all of our titles are available for purchase?

We publish a wide range of high quality large print books including:
Romances, Mysteries, Classics
General Fiction
Non Fiction and Westerns

Special interest titles available in large print are:
The Little Oxford Dictionary
Music Book, Song Book
Hymn Book, Service Book

Also available from us courtesy of Oxford University Press:
Young Readers' Dictionary
(large print edition)
Young Readers' Thesaurus
(large print edition)

For further information or a free brochure, please contact us at:
Ulverscroft Large Print Books Ltd.,
The Green, Bradgate Road, Anstey,
Leicester, LE7 7FU, England.
Tel: (00 44) **0116 236 4325**
Fax: (00 44) **0116 234 0205**

FORGOTTEN

Fay Cunningham

Driving home in the dark, Serena stops to help an injured man lying in a ditch. He mutters something unintelligible, but that is only the start of her problems. Someone is watching the apartment she shares with her brother, her mother is being particularly secretive, and police detective Jack Armstrong is convinced Serena is hiding something. Just when she thinks things can get no worse, her missing father turns up. This is definitely not the time to fall in love.

A PERFECT RHAPSODY

Dawn Bridge

After an unhappy romance with a concert pianist, Emma joins her local orchestra — something she has always wanted to do. Their new young conductor, Paul, seems to be an aloof and arrogant man, but Emma finds herself attracted to him. What secret is he concealing? Will she be able to break through the barrier which he has erected around himself? And how can she ever hope to compete with the beautiful Samantha for his affections, whilst dealing with admirers of her own?

TIDES OF LOVE

Phyllis Mallett

When her widowed father dies, Clarissa Marston is left penniless. George Farand, however, has a solution: in debt to the late Mr. Marston, he invites Clarissa to stay with his family at their Cornish estate of Trevarron until he can repay her the money. She warms to the genial John Farand, despite his darkly brooding brother Edwin. But Trevarron is a place of ominous secrets, and Clarissa begins to fear for her safety — until the handsome Richard Redmond comes to her aid . . .

FATE IN FREEFALL

Ken Preston

Paralysed by grief after losing her fiancé in a skydiving accident, Katrina Maslow cannot allow herself to love another man. She travels the world in an attempt to flee from her former life, ending up in Rio and accepting a job as a guide with J Stone Adventure Trips. But Jay, the handsome owner of the company, is determined to break down her reserves. As they are pursued by a ruthless killer, Katrina finally realises she is in love with Jay — just at the moment she might lose him forever . . .

THE TIGER IN MEN

Denise Robins

When Fenella Shaw left England to take possession of a Canadian cattle ranch in the Saskatchewan Valley, gifted to her as a legacy by her father, she quickly fell in love with handsome Max Geerling, the manager. It came as no surprise to anyone when the news of their engagement was announced, the neighbouring farmers believing them to be ideally matched. But Max is not all he seems to be — and Fenella finds herself caught up in a situation so alien to her that she fears she may never escape . . .